MW01503442

CYNTHIA HICKEY

Cowboy Christmas Crisis

Cynthia Hickey

The Cowboys of Misty Hollow

ISBN-13: 978-1-965352-19-9

Chapter One

Mackenzie Anderson's hand suspended her fork of lasagna halfway to her mouth. "What do you mean the mob wants you to work for them?" She stared at her brother Alex.

"Not the mob. A gang. Vincent Romano to be exact." He sat back against the booth. "He's told me things, Mack. Things I don't want to know. His dealings, who he's working with…" He shook his head. "By telling me those things, he believes I'll be forced to work with him. I won't."

"What will you do?" Her hand trembled, the lasagna falling back to her plate.

He reached across the table and took her free hand. "I need you to promise me something."

"Of course." Her mouth dried at the look of fear in his eyes.

"If something happens to me, I want you to go to Misty Hollow. Levi Owens works on the Rocking W Ranch. He'll help you."

Her fork clattered to the table. "You think something is going to happen?"

"With Romano, who knows?" He straightened.

"He wants to become a big-time crime boss and will do whatever it takes."

"Go to the police, Alex. You can't fight him off alone." Her eyes stung with tears.

"I'm probably being overcautious, but I thought you should know what I'm up against."

"You're scaring me." Appetite gone, she pushed her half-eaten meal to the side. "Nothing can happen to you. With Mom and Dad gone…" her voice broke. "You're all I have, Alex."

"I know, Sis." He grinned. "We're a team, you and I. Without your paralegal skills, I could have never become the lawyer I am. It'll be okay. Just keep your eyes open, will you?"

"Of course." Her hand shook as she reached for her glass of iced tea. "When did he contact you?"

"We've been talking for a few weeks."

"A few weeks! Alex, you should've said no right away." She glanced around the restaurant to see whether anyone paid them too much attention.

A man hid behind the menu. His dark eyes met hers for a moment before returning to the menu. His hair had been combed back, making it appear as if he had more hair than he did. A mother wiped the face of a small child who whimpered that he wanted to go home. Another man exited the restroom and sat at a table for one.

Alex shrugged. "I wanted to give the man the benefit of the doubt."

"What does he want your help with?"

"Anything that comes up. Romano wants me on his payroll. You, too, actually. That's when I backed off. There's no way I want you involved with a man like him."

"You shouldn't be either." Anger replaced fear. "You're smarter than that."

"The money would've been amazing."

"It's not always about the money." She wanted to shake some sense into him. When had money become more important to her brother than doing what was right? "I doubt Levi even remembers me."

"He's my best friend, Mack. I trust him more than anyone besides you. He'll watch out for you if it comes to that." Alex grew serious. "He and I talk at least once a week. Levi's happy being a cowboy, and I'm happy being a lawyer. It works for us."

"You haven't seen him in how long? What makes you think he's capable of protecting me?"

Alex's grin returned. "Since college. Levi spent some time as a private investigator after his time in the Marines. I trust him completely."

"Ten years ago." If the worst happened and she had to go to Levi, how would he react after so long? A PI Marine turned cowboy? "Let's change the subject. You're closing the office next week for vacation. Where are you going?"

"That's the funny thing." He laughed. "I'm going to Misty Hollow to do some hunting and fishing."

"It'll be cold."

"Yep. What about you?"

"I'm not going to do anything but enjoy the time off." Catch up on her reading, maybe do some home improvements, whatever she wanted to do when the mood struck.

"Let's get you home." Alex stood. "Sorry to ruin the mood during our weekly supper together." He tossed money on the table.

"You do know how to show a girl a good time." She tried to lighten the mood despite the cloud of doom hanging over the evening.

"Must be why I'm still single despite being devastatingly handsome."

Mack forced a laugh. "That would be because you're a workaholic and in love with yourself." She shrugged into her coat before looping arms with him. Their weekly Friday night supper should've been the kickoff to their vacation. Instead, Alex had ruined the joy of a week off work with his bad news. Sometimes her brother seemed so dense.

They exited the Italian restaurant into a slight drizzle. The November chill sent a shiver down Mack's spine, and she tugged the collar of her coat higher. Winter promised to be a bitter one that year.

Levi glanced at the sky. "The weather's turning bad. We'll have to hurry." He veered right behind some tall office buildings.

"Not the alley." Mack tugged him back. "The streetlight is out."

"We're going to be soaked if we take the long way." He grabbed her hand. "You don't want to spend your vacation sick, do you?"

"No." Her heart lodged in her throat. "Let's hurry then." She increased her pace, almost jogging to get out of the shadows.

A figure loomed in front of them, then another, and another.

Alex stepped in front of Mack. "Romano's thugs. Run." He whipped around and gave her a shove.

"Are you sure?" She couldn't tell anything about

them without light.

"Positive." He dragged her into a sprint.

Two more men stepped in front of them, blocking their escape.

"What do we do?" Mack shrank against her brother.

"I'll try and talk them into leaving us alone. You get out of here right away. I'll tell them I've decided to work for Romano."

"If they don't believe you?"

"Go to Levi." He pushed her behind a dumpster. "Hello, boys."

The gang immediately surrounded him.

Mack slipped from behind the dumpster and slunk along the brick wall toward the end of the alley. Once she had a bit of light, she pulled her cell phone from her coat pocket and dialed 911.

"A bunch of gang members are surrounding my brother." She kept her gaze locked on Alex who seemed to be in a heated debate with one of the men. "The alley behind the old bank on third street."

"Find a safe place and stay there," the operator said. "Police are on their way."

Mack gasped as one of the gang members pulled a knife and stabbed her brother. Again and again. "The guys have knives. They're killing him. Oh, God. Alex!"

The men turned in her direction.

Mack dropped her phone and darted from the alley as the men gave chase.

Sirens wailed in the distance.

Could it be soon enough to save her brother? Could he survive that many stab wounds? Tears blurred her vision. She'd fled like a frightened rabbit.

She glanced over her shoulder to see two of the men still giving chase. She screamed and raced into the street. Horns honked as cars swerved to avoid hitting her. She continued her mad dash until she burst into her condo.

Go to Levi kept repeating in her mind. She grabbed a suitcase from the top shelf of her closet and tossed in clothes, then her laptop and purse. She'd need a new phone. Misty Hollow would have phones for sale. She turned in a circle. What was she forgetting? *God, help me. God, help Alex.*

She covered her face with her hands. Was he still alive? She'd left him lying bleeding in the alley.

No. She had to go. There would be time to punish herself later. She'd made a promise to Alex. A promise to seek help from Levi.

Snatching her car keys from a hook near the back door, she raced to her car, dragging her suitcase behind her. She tossed it into the back seat. Seconds later, she backed from the drive and careened away from her condo, then she took the exit to Interstate 40 toward Misty Hollow.

All she knew about the town was it was somewhere in the Ozark mountains of Northern Arkansas. When she stopped for gas, she'd put in the Rocking W Ranch into her car's GPS...no, she'd dropped her phone in the alley. She'd have to stop for the night somewhere and buy a new phone first thing in the morning.

When her eyes fought to stay open, she rented a room in a rundown motel outside of Langley then parked her car behind some overgrowth near the parking lot to keep it out of sight of the highway.

Sleep didn't come easy. Instead, Mack lay on her back, eyes staring through the dim room at a water stain on the ceiling as she focused on her last sight of Alex. Her brother was stabbed at least three times, then fell to the cracked asphalt of the alley. The gang members gave chase when she'd stopped to glance back.

Had she lost them? After her parents died in a boating accident, Alex and Mack had made a promise always to look out for each other. Mack had failed him by running. She held onto a thread of hope that the police had arrived in time to save her brother, but that thread was as fine as frog hair. A call to local hospitals hadn't resulted in anyone matching Alex's description being brought in.

Her tears streamed through her hair onto the pillow. She rolled onto her side, hugging the lumpy pillow to her stomach. Grief sent pain through her as if she'd experienced the same knifing as Alex.

He couldn't be dead. Her brother was all she had left in the world. Instead of staying with him, she was running like a coward to seek safety with her brother's best friend. A man Mack hadn't seen in ten years. Not since she was fifteen.

Every sound outside her room had her tensing in anticipation of someone breaking through the motel door. She doubted the chair she'd propped under the doorknob would hold anyone out for long. Plus, the glass window could easily be shattered.

If she didn't feel the need for a phone, she'd have driven through the night and waited until daylight to reach the Rocking W Ranch. Too late now.

She'd abandoned Alex and fled to save her own life. How could she ever live with herself?

Answer—By seeking vengeance and making sure justice was served against the man responsible.

Chapter Two

The next morning, after a sleepless night plagued with visions of her brother's attack, Mack sat in her car outside the cell phone store and sent a hopeful text to her brother's phone letting him know she'd escaped Little Rock and would be in Misty Hollow in half an hour. She then put the ranch into her GPS and drove toward what she hoped would be the first step in her quest to avenge Alex.

The drive up Misty Mountain would have invited her to stop and enjoy the view if she didn't feel as if the hounds of hell were on her heels. Sending Alex a text could be a huge mistake if Romano had his phone. She'd run the risk of him knowing her exact destination. Still, if Alex was alive, she had to take the chance of letting him know she'd gotten away.

She drove up the long drive toward a large white house flanked by pastures with horses and cows. A big red barn stood on a hill with smaller outbuildings behind it along with a row of what looked like tiny cottages. A successful ranch at first glance, and it seemed secluded enough to provide the shelter Mack sought. At least she hoped so.

She stopped her car in front of the house and watched as cowboys milled in and out of the barn and pastures. She couldn't pick Levi out of the crowd, not with them all wearing cowboy hats that shaded their faces.

A blond woman stepped out of the house and waved to Mack from the front porch.

"Here goes nothing." Mack shoved open her car door and approached the woman. "Good morning. I'm looking for Levi Owens."

"Please tell me you aren't a damsel in distress." A thin, wiry cowboy stepped around the corner of the house. "Women bring trouble."

"Hush, Willy." The blond woman smiled. "I'm Dani Wyatt. You'll find Levi in the barn. Welcome to the Rocking W."

"Thank you." Casting a wary glance at the older cowboy, Mack headed for the barn.

Her heart beat in her throat. It had been a long time since she'd seen Levi. What if he sent her away? She had nowhere else to go and needed help making Romano pay for her brother's attack. Levi's law enforcement background would be a huge help.

She stepped into a cavernous barn with stalls stretching down both sides. Dust from hay being tossed over stall doors made her sneeze, and she reached for the inhaler she usually kept in her pocket only to discover she'd left it in her purse in the car.

Without announcing her presence to the man tossing the hay, she rushed back to her car, took two puffs of the inhaler, then returned to the barn with the inhaler in her pocket. She knew better than to go anywhere without it. Fear had made her foolish.

Her steps lagged as she approached the man now lugging a saddle toward one of the stalls. "Levi?"

He turned, his walnut-colored eyes widening. "Big Mack?" He glanced past her, a grin on his face. "I was expecting Alex. Did you decide to come with him?"

Tears sprang to her eyes, and she shook her head, trying to force an explanation from her throat. "He... he isn't coming."

Levi set the saddle on a hay bale and removed his hat. The sun had lightened his already ash blond hair to an even lighter hue. His smile faded. "What's wrong? Where is Alex?"

She plopped onto a three-legged stool. "He got into...trouble. We were attacked in an alley on our way home last night. He was stabbed."

He pulled her to her feet, hands on her upper arms. "Are you telling me Alex is dead?"

"I don't know." Her body shook with sobs. "He told me to run. To come here. That you would help me."

"And I will, but I need to know exactly what happened." He tilted her face to his. "Calm down and tell me, Big Mack."

"Don't call me that. I'm not the chubby little girl you once knew anymore." She stepped out of his grasp.

"No, you aren't." He led her to a rickety chair in the corner and took the stool for himself. "I'm listening."

She told him of their conversation at the restaurant—of her brother making her promise to go to Levi if anything happened. She described the attack and the men pursuing her home. "So, here I am."

"You have no idea whether Alex is alive or dead." It wasn't a question.

"No. I sent him a text letting him know—"

"That probably wasn't the smartest thing to do, Mackenzie." He stood and thrust his hands through his hair. "You'll have led this Romano fella straight to you."

"I had to let Alex know I'd made it." She couldn't have her injured brother worrying about her. Not if he was alive. "What's our next step?"

"Our next step? We can't go up against a gang boss." He narrowed his eyes. "I came to this ranch to get away from that stuff."

She bolted to her feet. "Not even to avenge your best friend?" She planted fists on her hips. "Are you afraid, Levi?"

~

Afraid? No. But after what he'd seen while a Marine, he wanted nothing more to do with danger and death. He turned and paced the barn. What was he supposed to do with his friend's little sister?

Not a pudgy child anymore. While she barely reached his shoulder when standing, the dark-haired little girl had grown into a beautiful woman with shining eyes the color of the summer sky.

Now, here she was wanting his help for the attack on her brother. "We need to find out whether Alex is alive or not. If he's dead, you can leave the whole thing alone."

"I won't." Obstinance crossed her face. "I'll make sure Romano pays for his death. If Alex is alive, then we need to find him and still bring Romano down."

"How do you propose we do that? Misty Hollow

is four hours away from the man."

She hitched her chin. "We find the evidence we need to put him behind bars. I've worked with Alex in his law office since college. I'm not completely without experience and neither are you. Are you going to help me or not?"

"Of course, I'm going to help you." He sighed. How could he not? If left to her own devices, Mack would end up like her brother. Levi wouldn't be able to live with himself. "Wait here. I'll talk to my boss about letting you stay in one of the tiny houses."

His boots crunched across gravel on his way to the main house. Inside, he knocked on the door of his boss, Dylan Wyatt, and waited to be called in.

Dylan looked up from the ledger in front of him. "What can I do for you, Levi?"

His boss's face set in grim lines as Levi repeated what Mack had told him. "I'm wondering whether she can stay, so I can keep an eye on her," Mack said.

"Why is it women bring trouble to this town? It's like a curse!" Dylan crossed his arms. "You know I won't send her away. This ranch is for people like her and wounded warriors. I have to admit to getting tired of trouble coming to where my family lives. It's worse with Christmas only a month away."

Levi understood. Dylan had sent his family away for their safety on more than one occasion. "I can take her to a hunting cabin. Wait things out there."

"No, there's safety in numbers. This isn't the first rodeo these ranch hands have been through, you know that. They'll rally around you. This woman can stay in number three and help with the housework when the two of you aren't gallivanting around trying to bring down a gang boss." He shook his head again. "Make sure she knows how to shoot."

"Okay." He had no idea since he hadn't seen or spoken to her since she was fifteen.

Back in the barn, he told Mack she could stay, then helped her carry her few items to house number three. "Let me introduce you to Marilyn and Mrs. White. You'll be helping them while you stay here."

"What about Romano?"

"We'll make time to do some digging." He set her suitcase inside the door of number three. "Everyone pitches in on this ranch, Mack."

"I don't have a problem with that." She sat on the sofa. "I appreciate getting to stay here, but I can't let Alex's attack be forgotten."

"It won't be. I said I'd help you and I will. Did you bring a laptop?"

"Yes."

"Then start by finding out everything you can online about Romano. Lunch is at noon, supper at six. Then breakfast tomorrow at six a.m. I'm sure Mrs. White will want you to help with the meals. Ready to meet her?"

Mack nodded and followed him from the house.

"Everyone here is used to folks seeking refuge on the ranch. You aren't alone here."

"That's good to know."

"Can you shoot?" He glanced back.

"A gun? Some." She paled. "You expect to get into a gunfight? This isn't the wild, wild west."

"No, but you might need to protect yourself."

"Or someone else. If I'd had a weapon, I could've protected Alex."

"What happened to him isn't your fault. He got into trouble by his own choices." If his friend was standing in front of him, Levi might punch him in the nose himself to try to knock some sense into his thick, stupid skull.

"You don't look any different in ten years. A little harder maybe," Mack said.

He chuckled. "You look different. You're all grown up."

"That tends to happen to people."

He held the back door open for her. "After you, darlin'."

"Oh, a cowboy drawl. Be still my heart." She gave a trembling smile. "Thank you again for saying you'll help me."

"How could I not, Big Mack." He grinned as her cheeks reddened.

"Stop calling me that. I developed a complex from your teasing." She brushed past him.

"Well, who is this?" Mrs. White dried her hands on a dishtowel.

"Mackenzie Anderson. Mack for short. She's the sister of a good friend of mine, and she'll be staying in house three for a while. Put her to work, ma'am." Levi planted a kiss on the woman's plump cheek. "There's no one I trust more to keep her under their wing."

"You are such a flirt, young man." She thrust out her hand to Mack. "It's nice to meet you. I can always use help with the cleanup after meals, if you don't mind."

"Not at all." Mack smiled.

Mrs. White tilted her head. "There's a story here, I think."

Mack shot him a quick glance. "Yes, but I'm not ready to make it public knowledge if that's okay."

"Sure, it is. It'll all come out eventually anyway. See you at noon." Mrs. White pulled a bowl from the cupboard and started measuring ingredients.

"The boss is next," Levi said. "Don't worry. His wife has a story similar to yours."

"Really?"

"Yep. Everyone on the Rocking W has a story of some sort. Either they were in danger, wounded, or suffer from PTSD. That's what this place is. A refuge."

He hoped that's what it would be for her. A safe place, not a trap.

Chapter Three

More than one curious glance was cast Mack's way at lunch. She set a large platter of sloppy joe sandwiches in the center of the table. Seeing one of the twins frowning at her, she offered a smile. "What did I do?"

"Every time a new girl comes to the ranch, we have to leave." The boy grabbed a sandwich. "Because the girl brings trouble with a capital T. Then, she marries one of our ranch hands, and we have to hire another one." He narrowed his eyes at her. "Are you going to do that, too?"

Mack's mouth opened and closed like a gasping fish. Her face heated as laughter rang out around the table. She glanced at Levi's amused expression as he bit into a sandwich. "No, I, uh…" She turned and fled to the kitchen.

Once there, she planted her hands flat on the counter and hung her head. What had Alex been thinking to send her to the ranch? Sure, he trusted Levi, and Mack found herself surrounded by cowboys toting guns on their hips, but there were children here. The twin was right about one thing. She would bring trouble to the Rocking W.

"Don't worry, dear." Mrs. White put a hand on her shoulder. "They're only teasing. Best get used to it. That's a silly bunch out there."

"I shouldn't have come."

"You aren't the first damsel in distress to say those words, and it all turned out okay in the end. Have faith. Here. Refill the tea, then sit down and eat something. You don't weigh more than a minute." The woman thrust a pitcher of iced tea into her hands.

"What do I do after lunch?"

"Once the dishes are done, you're free until I need you for supper. Marilyn is going to take a few days off since you're here to help me. Go on now." Mrs. White shooed her away.

Good. That would give Mack a few hours to do some more research on her laptop. She needed to know everything there was to find on Vincent Romano. Mack could also have their receptionist, Sarah, do some digging. Information would be key to putting a stop to his growing empire.

She carried the pitcher into the dining room and refilled glasses before setting it down and taking her seat. Someone had put a sandwich and a handful of fries on her plate. "Thank you."

"If I didn't," Levi said, "there wouldn't have been anything left for you. This is a greedy bunch."

This wasn't the first time he'd done something thoughtful. Growing up, he'd often come to her rescue when Alex picked on her to the point of making her cry. Seeing that he still had the tendency to do that brought tears to her eyes. "Thank you," she said again softly.

"Anything for Alex's little sister." He grinned,

keeping the mood light. "Eat up. We've got things to do this afternoon."

She jerked her head up. "Like what?"

"Digging for clues, Big Mack."

"Why do you call her that?" One of the twins asked. Mack really needed to learn their names and how to tell them apart.

"Because she's always been such a little thing." Levi chuckled.

"I hate that nickname."

"And that's why you'll always be called Big Mack." One of the ranch hands, Maverick the foreman, she thought, pointed a french fry in her direction. "Tip number one. Never let this bunch know how to get under your skin."

"Thanks for the warning." Mack squeezed a pile of ketchup on her plate. She'd never been one to take teasing well. Although she wasn't a pudgy little girl anymore, that hateful nickname dug it all back up. Maybe she should tell Levi how his nickname made her feel.

"Welcome to the ranch." The owner, Dylan, entered the room with his wife. "Levi, after lunch, I'd like to see you and Miss Anderson in my office."

Was she in trouble already? Some of her anxiety ebbed at the warm smile from the boss's wife, but why would she be summoned so soon? Unless he wanted to know more about why she'd come to his ranch. That had to be what he wanted.

She kept quiet during the meal, listening as the others discussed the day's chores. Levi seemed to be more of a mechanic on the ranch judging by what he'd been assigned to do. A tractor needed fixing. She guessed they couldn't all be on horseback, breaking broncs, or whatever it was that modern-day cowboys did.

She ate quickly and helped clear the table before following Levi to the boss's office.

"Don't worry." Levi knocked on the door. "The boss doesn't bite. He's one of the fairest men I know."

She nodded and entered a room lined with bookcases, mahogany furniture, and red and green striped fabric. Beautiful and masculine. "Sir."

"No need for formalities. I'm Dylan." He motioned to a chair. "Have a seat, please."

"Then you must call me Mack." She perched on the edge of a chair, Levi taking the one next to her.

"Levi told me why you're here, and you're welcome. This is a place of refuge. Any one of these ranch hands will have your back if needed." He folded his hands on top of his desk. "I've received some news from the sheriff."

"You told him about me?" Mack widened her eyes.

"Of course. This is his town. Sheriff Westbrook is a good man and deserves to know. He called me right before lunch to let me know there's been a swarm of newcomers to Misty Hollow not counting you."

"How many?" Levi asked.

"At least five that he's seen. Doesn't mean there's not more."

"Any idea where they're holing up?"

Dylan shook his head. "But he does want to speak to Mack."

Her hands trembled as she pushed to her feet. "Then, we'd best go see him." Sending a text to her brother's phone had been a big mistake.

~

Levi held the passenger door to his truck open for Mack. She slid in, a worried gaze on her face. "I didn't expect them to come so soon."

"They must've come right after you texted Alex." He closed the door and jogged to the driver's side. Inside, he turned to her. "Best to get it over with, right? If it is Romano and his men, they'll be easier to keep an eye on."

"And out of Little Rock, so I can search my brother's office."

He started to protest, then realized she was right. They would need access to Alex's office in order to find anything concrete on Romano. "Do not do anything alone, Mack. I mean it." He turned the key in the ignition and drove away from the ranch.

"I'm not a little kid that you can order around anymore."

"No, you're not, but you said yourself that Alex told you to come to me. That means he's trusting me to watch out for you. I can't do that if you take off on your own."

"Remember the time I got lost following you and Alex into the woods when the two of you went camping?" She gave a sad smile. "You found me then. Saved me from drowning because I'd try to cross a creek and got stuck on a rock. Looks like you might have to save me again."

He reached over and gave her hand a squeeze. "I'll always be here for you, Big Mack. Always. You and Alex."

"You think he's alive?" Hope shone in her eyes.

"Until I know otherwise, I'm going to believe he is. If his body was found, the sheriff will know."

"Okay. I'm going to hold onto hope, too." She stared out the window. "This is a beautiful place."

"I'll show you how the town got its name sometime."

"I'd like that."

He pointed out places of interest as they entered the city. The diner, coffee shop, drugstore, mercantile, and grocery store. "If you're a big reader, the bookstore in the coffee shop always has the latest new releases. Plus, there's quite a library at the ranch."

"I do enjoy reading and didn't have time to grab any of my books when I left."

He pulled in front of the red-brick sheriff's office. "Ready?"

Mack nodded and shoved her door open, not waiting for him. She squared her shoulders and marched toward the front door.

Petite but strong was Mackenzie Anderson. She'd be all right. Levi would make sure of that. He grabbed the door before she could and ushered her into the warmth of the building.

"You don't have to open doors for me."

"My mother will come out of her grave and whip me if I'm not a gentleman." He grinned before letting the receptionist know the sheriff was expecting them.

She spoke into her phone, then motioned them down the hall. "First door on the right."

The sheriff stood from behind his desk and offered his hand to each of them for a shake. "Have a seat." He sat and locked his gaze on Mack. "Levi and Dylan told me a little about why you're here, Miss

Anderson, but I'd like to hear the details from you."

She repeated what she'd told Levi upon her arrival. Had it really only been that morning?

"The text you sent gave away your location." The sheriff didn't look pleased.

"Yes, sir, but I had to let Alex know I was okay if…he's still alive."

"I've contacted LRPD, and no one matching your brother's description has been found alive or dead. Let's assume he's alive at this point." Sheriff Westbrook crossed his arms. "My deputies are searching to find out where our new arrivals are staying. It isn't at the motel. Romano isn't stupid. He'll have rented a secluded house. We'll find him. In the meantime, I want you to stay at the Rocking W where you have protection."

She shook her head. "I'll be looking for evidence to bring Romano down. I'm a paralegal. My brother's a lawyer. I know how to dig deep." Stubbornness laced her words.

The sheriff transferred his attention to Levi. "You have law enforcement background. Do you plan on helping her?"

"It's what my friend wanted." He gave a nod. "I know Mack well enough to know she'll go searching with or without me. It's safer if I'm with her."

"Don't do anything illegal." The sheriff frowned.

"I have a key to my brother's office. Since I work there, I have every right to enter, and since the stabbing took place in the alley, his office is not a crime scene."

Sheriff Westbrook chuckled. "Correct. I'll keep you informed on anything I learn and ask that you do the same for me. Deal?" He offered his hand again.

Mack gave him a firm shake. "Deal."

Levi also shook on the deal, then escorted Mack back to his truck. "Anything you need while we're in town?"

She sat for a moment, then nodded. "Since I have no idea how long I'll be staying on the ranch, I should pick up a few toiletries and other personal items. Is there a supermarket or department store close?"

"Yep." He drove them to a large supercenter. "You'll find everything you need in here."

Half an hour later with more bags than Levi thought Mack should need, they headed back to the ranch. "Want to go to Little Rock this evening?"

"Really?" Her eyes widened. "That would be great. I could stop by my—"

"Nope. Not going by your place. They'll be watching it."

Her brow furrowed. "They'll be watching the office, too."

"True, but going to two places is more dangerous than one, in my opinion. We hit the office during the night, do some searching, and get out quick. The longer we're in the big city, the greater the danger. Anyone you need to notify?"

"Sarah, but she works days. I do need to let her know the office will be closed until further notice." She dug her phone from her pocket and sent a text. "I don't want her anywhere near the danger."

"You're a good woman, Big Mack."

"Yeah. So good I ran while my brother was being stabbed." She turned away from him.

Chapter Four

They left right after supper to begin the over-four-hour drive to Little Rock.

"We should've left sooner," Levi said. "I'd like to question Alex's neighbors, the offices around his—"

Mack jerked to face him. "We could stop for the night, then spend the day tomorrow questioning people before searching his office after dark. That would give me time to get a hold of Sarah. She hasn't responded to my text messages." Which was not like their receptionist at all.

"I'll have to let Dylan know we won't be back by morning, but I'm sure he'll be fine with it." Levi turned his attention back to the road.

"Can I tell you something?" Finally, she would get it off her chest how much his nickname for her hurt.

"Anything. You know that."

She took a deep breath before speaking. "I hate being called Big Mack."

He shot her a questioning glance. "It bothers you?"

"Yes. As a former chubby kid—"

"You weren't chubby!" He frowned. "What

makes you think you were'?"

"Alex said I was." Multiple times.

"That was just the teasing of an older brother." He reached over and patted her leg. "Mack, I call you Big Mack because like the hamburger I always wanted, you're one of my favorite things. It's a term of endearment, not a slam." He returned his hand to the steering wheel. "I won't call you that anymore."

A term of endearment? Really? Her face heated. How she would've loved to have heard those words come out of his mouth years ago. She'd had a crush on him as big as Mount Everest. "Now that I know what you mean, the name doesn't hold the same sting." She smiled.

"I still won't call you that anymore."

"Do you still eat Big Macs?"

"Not as much." He flashed a grin. "I've replaced that obsession with working on farm equipment and riding horses."

She returned his smile. "Good thing, or you would've been the pudgy one now."

They spent the rest of the drive reminiscing. Mack dozed off a few times, glad when Levi stopped at a motel outside Little Rock. He rented a room with two queen beds. Mack fell onto hers as soon as she took off her shoes.

When she woke the next morning to discover Levi had pulled a blanket over her, she glanced at his bed. Empty. The sound of the shower running let her know he'd beaten her to the bathroom.

She shuffled to the provided coffeepot, pour water into it, and turned it on while she waited for her turn. Not having intended to spend the night anywhere, she didn't have any clean clothes to change into. Still, a shower would feel nice and help her wake up ready to start gathering clues to what had happened to Alex.

She refused to lose hope. Her brother had to be alive and in hiding, otherwise there would've been mention of his death on the news, right?

"Your turn." Levi, hair wet from his shower, stepped from the bathroom. "Coffee. Yay. I should've started it before hitting the shower, I guess."

"No problem." She lumbered to the bathroom.

"Still not a morning person, huh?"

"Nope." She closed the door firmly and turned on the water.

"I want you to show me the alley where Alex was attacked," Levi said through the door.

"Okay." She stepped under the spray, trying to get a few moment's peace to wake up. Levi and her brother were morning people, and both started yakking the moment their eyes opened. It had always driven her crazy.

After her shower, she poured herself a cup of coffee and sat at the small table in the room while Levi left to find something for breakfast, giving her a few minutes to wake up. By the time he returned with breakfast burritos from a nearby Mexican restaurant, she was on her second cup and ready to start the day.

"The alley first, then we start asking questions." Levi sat across from her. "That should fill up the day until nightfall. Then, we break into—"

"We don't have to break in. I have a key."

"Right. Sorry." He finished his breakfast, then stood and reached into a convenience store bag. ."I stopped and bought toothbrushes, toothpaste, and a comb."

"You're my hero." She smiled, grabbed the toiletries, and made a mad dash back to the bathroom.

A few minutes later, she stood at the entrance to the alley. Crime scene tape fluttered from where it had hung up on a pile of garbage. Mack's heart beat in her throat. Perspiration dotted her upper lip despite the chilly November day. "There. By the dumpster is where Alex was stabbed."

"You stay here. I'll check things out myself." He gave her a concerned gaze, then headed for the spot she'd mentioned.

~

Levi wasn't sure what he'd find, if anything, but his prior job as MP gave him an edge an average man wouldn't have. He skirted a stain on the pavement that looked like blood, then slipped behind the dumpster. Mack had said she'd lost her phone. If he didn't find it, he'd bet his hat that Romano's thugs had.

Of course, a homeless person could've snatched it and sold it for a few dollars, but the men who attacked Alex would've gotten to it first. Not finding the phone or any clue as to where Alex might've gone, he returned to Mack.

"Anything on your phone that might help Romano?" He asked.

"No. Just contacts, clients, but nothing about any of the cases. No details anyway." She tilted her head. "You think he has my phone?"

Levi nodded. "He might be interested in the contacts. Since Alex turned him down, he could be on the lookout for another lawyer to add to his payroll."

"My brother's files would have more information.

The office building has tight security. Without a key and the code, it would be hard for anyone to get in once office hours were over."

"Okay. Let's head to his neighborhood."

Back in the car, he listened as Mack recited her brother's address, then punched it into his GPS. They should be there in fifteen minutes.

"I doubt many people will be home. He lives in an apartment complex of other business-type people."

"We might get lucky." He drove to the swanky, modern building. His friend seemed to have done well for himself, judging by the building and models of expensive vehicles in the parking lot. His truck looked like a rust stain on fresh porcelain.

He glanced at his faded jeans. Oh, well. He was who he was. Levi opened the truck door and firmly planted his scuffed cowboy boots on the ground. Who cared what he wore? He was there to help Mack find Alex, not win a chance to be on the cover of a magazine.

"What's wrong?" Mack frowned.

"Nothing." He marched toward the glass doors and stared at a code box. "I don't know the code."

Mack reached around him and punched it in. The doors slid open with a whoosh. "You woke up in a relatively good mood. What happened?"

"I'm being uncharacteristically self-conscious."

She laughed. "Oh, please. The confident, handsome Levi Owens feeling self-conscious?"

Just like that his bad mood evaporated. "You think I'm handsome?"

"Stop it. You know you are. Do you want to start at the bottom and work up to the second floor, or start up and work down?"

"What floor did Alex live on?"

"Second."

"Let's start there." He doubted they'd uncover anything, but a good investigator questioned neighbors. Sometimes, a man got lucky.

They knocked on five doors before someone answered. A woman dressed in a suit and heels answered. "I'm in a hurry." Her cool gaze swept over Levi, then warmed, and she smiled. "But, I can spare a minute or two. What do you need?"

He grinned, ready to lay on the charm if need be. "I'm Levi Owens, and this is Mackenzie Anderson, sister to your neighbor Alex."

"Haven't seen him in a couple of days." Her gaze flicked to Mack. "Is he all right?" Worry shadowed her features.

"Did you know my brother well?"

She nodded. "We've been dating about a month. My name is Rebecca Miller." She said it as if they were supposed to recognize the name. "It isn't like him not to call me. I thought maybe, he…well, I thought he'd moved on. I even called his receptionist, but she couldn't, or wouldn't tell me anything."

"We're trying to find out what happened to him. Did he ever mention somewhere he went to get away?" Mack asked.

The woman's smooth brow furrowed. "He mentioned wanting to take me to Eureka Springs, but that obviously didn't happen."

"Did he ever mention Misty Hollow or me, Levi?"

She shook her head. "Not that I remember. He is in trouble, isn't he?"

"Did he ever mention Vincent Romano?" Levi didn't want to frighten the woman, but if Alex had told her anything, then she might be in danger.

"He was contemplating working for the man. The money would be outstanding." She crossed her arms. "In fact, I have a meeting with Romano in half an hour. I'm sure he's going to ask me to be his lawyer if Alex is gone. Please tell me what happened to your brother."

"I suggest you not go to that meeting, Rebecca." Mack reached a hand toward her. "Get out of town. My brother was attacked and stabbed a couple of days ago by Romano's men."

"What?" Shock swept over her. "No, that's impossible. Vincent is a kind man. He does a lot of good for the community."

Levi widened his eyes. Were they talking about the same man? "What makes you say that?"

"I've done my research, Mr. Owens." She hitched her chin.

"I suggest you dig deeper, Miss Miller. Romano is nothing more than a wannabe crime boss. Working for him will only get you killed."

Her hand flew to her throat. "Is Alex dead?"

"That's what we're trying to find out. Be careful, ma'am." He placed a hand on the small of Mack's back and led her back to the truck.

"That's it? We aren't going to question anymore of the neighbors?"

"I want to see where she goes."

"We can't face Romano. No way. We aren't equipped."

"I didn't say anything about facing him. It doesn't hurt to see where he's holed up."

"Not in Misty Hollow?"

"The sheriff didn't mention him, only some of his men."

He kept his attention locked on the apartment doors. When the woman came out, she glanced both ways, then rushed to a silver Mercedes without sparing his old truck a look. Maybe a little rust among the glitz got overlooked sometimes.

"I cannot believe that woman is contemplating working for Romano." Mack leaned forward, craning her neck as the Mercedes sped from the parking lot. "And what was all that bull about how wonderful the man is?"

"She's obviously delusional. Blinded by the money, maybe." He tailed her, taking care to always keep a car between them and her.

She stopped outside a fancy Japanese restaurant, parked, then strode inside.

"We definitely aren't dressed for that place." Mack glanced at her jeans. "They wouldn't let us in."

"Sure they would, but, we would definitely attract attention. Since she said she was meeting Romano, we can safely assume he's still in Little Rock."

"And he sent his men to Misty Hollow to find me."

"Yes. Let's hope Miller doesn't mention she spoke to us."

"If she does, he'll come after me while we're here investigating." She paled. "We can't dig for information and watch our backs at the same time."

"Let's head back to the hotel and wait until dark." Staying off the streets would keep them safe if Miller did mention them. If no one saw him or Mack, Romano

might think they'd headed back to Misty Hollow.
He hoped.

Chapter Five

At ten p.m., Mack punched in the security code on the door of Alex's office, then inserted her key. Glancing up and down the hall, she opened the door.

"Let me go first." Levi clicked on a flashlight and stepped inside, Mack close on his heels.

She closed the door behind them with a gentle click, then turned on the flashlight in her other hand. The beam cut through the darkness. The room smelled of paper and leather with the faint aroma of her brother's cologne lingering in the air. A box of Christmas decorations sat in the corner waiting to be used.

"Anything look out of place?" Levi asked.

"Not that I can tell." Her brother was a bit of a neat freak when it came to his office. A direct contrast to his apartment, which was the next place on their list to comb through. "At least it doesn't look like anyone has been here since we left Friday night."

"Any idea where he keeps his files?"

"Over here." Mack led the way to a filing cabinet that matched the mahogany desk. She fished keys from her pocket. "I do most of his filing and don't recall ever seeing anything mentioning Romano. Sarah also files, but Alex kept her to the less important cases."

"If she files, though, she has access to everything in this cabinet, right?"

"Yes." She shined the light in his face, then lowered it when he shot a hand in front of his eyes. "Sorry. Sarah was vetted before my brother hired her. Alex didn't want to risk confidentiality for his clients."

"I'm not accusing her, just mentioning the fact that she might have seen something you missed." He set his flashlight on top of the cabinet and opened the drawer. "I doubt the file will say Romano. Does Alex use any kind of code in his filing?"

"No." Mack sat in the office chair and started opening drawers. The bottom right required a key she didn't have.

Hopefully, Alex hadn't had the key on him when he was attacked. She dug through his paper clips and middle "junk" drawer. Not finding a key, she sat back and tapped her fingers on the desk blotter. If she was Alex, where would she hide something small? Her gaze fell on the coffee mug holding pens.

She smiled and turned the mug upside down. Pens rolled across the desk. Taped to the bottom of the mug was a small key. She unlocked the drawer and riffled through the files there. These files were more sensitive than the ones Levi looked through. Still none of them shouted Romano, although some of the political names raised her eyebrows a notch.

As she moved the last file, her flashlight lit on a small indentation in the bottom corner. She pressed and revealed a false bottom. Inside lay a manila envelope with the name Romano scrawled across the front of it. "Bingo!"

A noise sounded outside the door. Both she and Levi clicked off their flashlights in unison. They sat so silently Mack could hear herself breathe.

The door cracked open. The form of a woman stood against the low light in the hall. "Alex?"

"No, it's me." Mack stood, blinking against the glare of the light Sarah flipped on.

"What are you doing here so late?" The receptionist glanced from her to Levi. "And why are you in the dark?" Her gaze landed on the envelope on the desktop.

Mack forced a smile. "I'm trying to find out where my brother might've disappeared to."

"In the dark?" Sarah frowned.

"We didn't want to alert the police if they drove by. What are you doing here?"

"I forgot a receipt I'd stuck in my desk. When I saw the flicker of a light under the door, I came to see if Alex had come in. To be honest I was starting to get worried. I know you said the office would be closed for a few days, but you didn't say why, and your brother is always here."

"He told me he was planning a vacation. Sarah, this is my brother's childhood friend, Levi." Mack tucked the file under her arm and headed for the door. "I thought maybe I could find out where he was going since he failed to mention that fact. I have some questions about one of the cases he has me working on." Mack stepped into the hall, followed by Levi.

Sarah locked the door after them. "He didn't tell me anything. If you're sure he's okay, then I won't worry anymore."

"Why wouldn't he be okay?" Sarah's not knowing

about the attack gave Mack a little more hope that Alex might have gone into hiding and survived the stabbing. If not, shouldn't there have been something on the news?

"It's just not like him." Sarah followed them to the front door.

"Take a few days off," Mack said. "I'll text you when I return to the office."

"Should I go ahead and decorate for the holidays?"

"Wait until we're back at work." Mack flashed what she hoped was a reassuring smile before following Levi to his truck.

Inside, they both stared through the front windshield at Sarah who stood watching them.

"Something seems off about her repeatedly asking if Alex is okay," Levi said. "You know her better than I do, but it didn't feel right."

"Yep. Almost like she fished for information as to whether Alex was alive." If it would've been anyone but Sarah asking the questions, Mack wouldn't have been suspicious, but Alex's receptionist had always been aloof and quiet. She did her job without getting personal.

~

"Alex's place?" Levi started the truck.

"Yes. I know you said you didn't want to go to my apartment, but there's something I need from there. I'm sure Romano thinks we've returned to Misty Hollow, if he even knew we'd come back to Little Rock."

"Okay." He backed from the parking spot. "Remember the adventures Alex and I used to go on?"

"The trouble you got into, you mean?" She laughed. "I tagged right along with you whenever the two of you took pity on me and let me join."

"There was one time when we were seniors in high school when you didn't come along." He cut her a sideways glance. "I think I might know where Alex is hiding."

"What?" Her eyes widened, shimmering in the glow of a streetlight.

"On senior ditch day, we took a couple of girls out by Lake Quachita and stayed in an abandoned cabin. Alex had said that someday he would buy a house on the lake."

"He's never mentioned buying a house to me."

"Doesn't mean he didn't. Did he always tell you everything?"

"Obviously not."

He drove her to her place first and waited in the truck while she ran inside and came out with a bag. "What's so important?"

"Alex's calendar. I always kept a copy." She tossed the bag behind the seat. "The lake first or his apartment?"

"The lake." He had a strong hunch they'd find something there.

It took a while before he found the cabin they'd once spent the night in. The building had been renovated.

"It doesn't look vacant or run-down." Mack peered through the windshield at a one-story cabin with a single garage. Behind the cabin Mack could see a dock leading out onto the lake.

"No, so let's hope Alex really did buy the place."

Levi slid his door open and took measured steps toward the house.

No cars sat parked in the long driveway or in the garage. He cupped his hands around his eyes and let his eyes adjust to the gloom inside at what appeared to be a living room. Simply furnished and dark. He moved to the back of the house, peering in every window. No one was home. "Look for a key."

"No need." She pushed open the back door.

"Stay behind me." Levi turned on his flashlight and entered a small but modern kitchen.

"This is breaking and entering." She placed a hand on his back.

"Yep. Make sure we leave everything as is, in case we determine Alex hasn't been here. Let's see whether there's a home office. Anything we need to know should be in there." He led the way down a short hall, shining his light into each room as they passed.

He paused in the door of the bathroom. "Mack." Bloody bandages, a needle and thread, and a bottle of antiseptic sat on the sink. "I think it's safe to say he was here."

"He's alive." Her voice broke as tears brimmed and fell down her cheeks.

Levi pulled her into his arms, resting his chin on top of her head. "Yes." Tears burned his own eyes.

She stepped back, raising red-rimmed eyes to his. "Where do you think he went from here?"

"I have no idea." He sighed. "Let's go to his apartment. He won't be there, but maybe we'll find something that will tell us where he's gone."

An hour later, they stood in Alex's apartment. "Why didn't we check here hours ago?"

"Because his girlfriend would've alerted Romano." Levi once again turned on his flashlight. "Besides, we followed her, remember?"

"I feel like we're running in circles."

"Probably because we are." He headed for the back of the apartment until he located Alex's home office.

The room resembled his work office, only on a smaller scale. No file cabinet stood in the corner. Levi sat at the desk and opened the largest drawer. "At least he doesn't keep his files locked up here."

"Which means he doesn't keep anything of importance here." Mack parted the blinds on the window. "I'm more nervous being here than I've been all night. What if Rebecca comes back? What if she sees us leave? Romano will know we're in town for sure."

"We can't not look. Not after coming all this way." Levi checked every drawer and found nothing. He flipped pages on the desk blotter, then picked it up. A sheet of paper lay underneath with Mack's name at the top. "He left you a letter."

She turned away from the window. "Read it."

Mack,

If you've found this, then it means something happened to me and you've gone to Levi. The two of you are looking into the trouble I've gotten myself involved in. I wish you wouldn't, but I know how you two are.

Vincent Romano will be behind whatever happened to me. I don't have proof. The man manages to commit his crimes while staying clean, using others to do his dirty work. Once I realized that, I knew I couldn't work for him. That would be my downfall, of course, but I haven't completely lost my morals.

Look into a man named Stephen Watson. He's a big real estate mogul. He's tied into Romano somehow. I think the two are in business together cutting corners on buildings.

Romano is a small-time crook who aspires to be a big-time crime boss. He is not to be trusted. Watch your back, little sister, and stay away from Little Rock.

Alex

"He's given us something to work with." Levi folded the note and stuck it in his pocket. "This and the file you found on Romano is a very good start."

Mack nodded and turned back to the window. "Levi, see that man over there by the streetlight? I think that man was at the restaurant the night Alex was attacked. I caught him watching us over the top of his menu."

"Are you sure?"

"Positive. I recognize the strange way he combs his hair over. He could be the one who let Romano know where we were that night."

"Then we need to find out who he is."

By the time Mack got to the window, the man had vanished.

Chapter Six

Mack managed to squeeze in a couple of hours of sleep before needing to help prepare lunch. Thankfully, Mrs. White had been gracious enough to allow her to skip breakfast.

In desperate need of coffee, she stepped onto the postage-size porch of the house she stayed in. A white envelope lay on the doormat, her name scrawled across the front.

She opened it and pulled out a single sheet of paper. Typed in bold font were the words, *Stop snooping around or pay the price. You have no idea who you're dealing with.*

Her hand shook as she glanced around the expansive grounds of the ranch. She looked up, noting the security camera. Whoever had left the note would be on film. Mack jumped from the porch and went in search of Levi. She'd apologize to Mrs. White for being late once she found out who had left the warning.

After asking a couple of ranch hands for Levi's whereabouts, she headed to a white metal building used as a mechanic shop on the ranch. Levi's scuffed boots showed from under a Ford truck.

"Someone left me a note."

Levi rolled from under the truck, his dark eyes covered by goggles. "What?"

She thrust the note at him. "I found this on my porch."

He wiped his greasy hands on a an equally dirty rag before taking the note. His brow furrowed as he read it. "We need to check the camera footage, then call the sheriff."

"Maybe it's the same guy I saw outside Alex's apartment." She had to jog to keep up with him as he marched to the main house and straight into Dylan's office. He looked surprised.

Levi quickly explained what had happened, then he and Mack watched over the boss's shoulder as he brought up the morning's security feed. They watched as Willy knocked on Mack's door, then placed the envelope on her doormat.

"Isn't he one of your workers?" Mack frowned.

"Yep. Wait here." Dylan strode from the office, returning a few minutes later with the older ranch hand.

"I'm sorry, Miss Anderson. Some guy drove up and stopped right inside the main gate. I went to see what he needed, and he asked me to deliver the note." He twisted the brim of his cowboy hat in his hands. "I didn't see any harm in it."

"What did he look like?" Levi asked.

"Dark hair, dark eyes. Hispanic, maybe. No trace of an accent, though." He glanced from Mack to Levi. "I really am sorry."

"That's okay." Mack sighed. "So, it wasn't the man we saw." What would the one delivering the note have done if no one would've gone to greet him? He couldn't have simply strolled up to the house without raising questions. At least this place took notice of visitors.

"So, it begins." Dylan rubbed his hands down his face. "I'm not sending my family away again."

"What do you propose?" Levi glanced his way.

"I bought plans to build a safe room off the pantry. It'll stretch behind the stairs. Guess I'll get workers here to start on it right away."

A safe room? Mack's blood chilled. "You think trouble will come to the ranch? With all the men you have working here?"

"It's happened a few times before. I'm not taking any chances this time. I'm also installing a gate at the ranch entrance. One that requires either a code to open or to be opened by someone in the house." Dylan reached for the phone on his desk. "This doesn't look like we'll be enjoying a peaceful Christmas."

"Anyone can just walk up from the main road, Boss." Willy shook his head. "The paddock fence isn't built to keep folks out, just to keep the livestock in. Plus, there's the woods…"

"Yes, but it'll keep people from driving up. Slow them down, maybe. With such security measures, they might think twice about starting trouble on my ranch. I'll see y'all at lunch."

Dismissed, the three filed from his office.

"I shouldn't have gone, despite Alex's wishes." All Mack had done was involve others in the danger she found herself in.

"Don't be ridiculous." Levi scowled. "You can't do this on your own. If you'd have stayed in Little Rock, you'd have suffered the same fate as Alex…or worse."

"But none of you would be in danger." She crossed her arms.

Willy cleared his throat and rushed away, no doubt anticipating the upcoming argument Mack knew was coming and wanting nothing to do with it.

Levi's face darkened. "You think that facing Romano alone and getting yourself killed is the answer?"

"Of course not. I wouldn't face Romano. I'm not that stupid. All I'm doing is trying to find enough information on the man to put him behind bars and stop him from rising to power."

"Can you two argue somewhere else?" Dylan called from his office. "I'm trying to work."

Levi gripped Mack's arm and led her outside. "I'm not letting you do this alone. Alex trusts me to protect you. I have the skills to do so."

She yanked free. "I never said I didn't want your help. All I said was I should never have come here and brought trouble with me. Now I need to go help Mrs. White with lunch. I've left her alone too long." She turned to go.

"Mack."

"I'm done talking, Levi. See you later." Without looking back, she headed to the back of the house and entered through the back door. "Sorry I'm late." She pulled an apron from a hook on the wall.

"Heard there was some ruckus," the other woman said. "I'm sure they heard you and Levi down in the valley."

"He misunderstood me."

"Men usually do. Especially when it comes to protecting their women. They get pigheaded." Mrs.

45

White faced her. "Coming here was not a mistake, Mackenzie. This is a safe place. These cowboys will all have your back. Be glad that Levi is one of them."

"I know. He's always been my protector ever since we were kids." She really wouldn't have it any other way. If only they could have reconnected under different circumstances. She wouldn't be able to live with herself if something happened to Levi because she'd done what her brother asked.

~

Why was Mack being so hardheaded? Levi rolled back under the vehicle he'd been working on earlier, then remembered neither one of them had called the sheriff. He rolled back out and made the call.

"I'm sure everyone and their grandmother has touched that note," Sheriff Westbrook said. "Hold onto it. I'll be by later, or you can drop it off at the office."

"I'll see whether Mrs. White needs anything from town. If she does, I'll stop by and leave it at the receptionist desk." Levi hung up and headed for the house as the lunch bell rang. At this rate, he'd never finish the repairs on the truck they used to haul feed.

Mack didn't meet his gaze as she set a plate of sloppy joe sandwiches in the center of the table. Nor did she look his way when she brought the fried potatoes.

He sighed, hating the fact he'd made her angry, but her statement that she shouldn't have come rubbed him the wrong way. Of course, she should have! Alex had been right to send her. Levi could protect her better than anyone. He'd known her since she was a young thing.

Despite not having an appetite, he filled his plate.

Usually, he devoured anything Mrs. White cooked. But, that was before he'd argued with Mack. He hoped they'd never disagree again. The argument had been a punch to his gut. "Need anything from town, Mrs. White?"

"I have a list. Thank you, Levi. Take Mackenzie with you."

Mack's head jerked his way. From her expression, it was obvious she had no desire to go into town with him.

"The sheriff wants me to drop off the note you received." He bit into his sandwich.

"Fine." She took a seat at the other end of the table.

After lunch, they climbed into his truck, still not speaking. It was going to be a long drive into town.

He decided to break through the chill that had little to do with the wintery day. "Can't you see my reasoning?"

She faced him. "Yes. I don't need heavy handling, Levi. We're partners in this. Alex is wounded and hiding. He can't come out until Romano is behind bars. All I said was that I shouldn't have come to the ranch. I never said that I wouldn't have contacted you."

"You didn't say that."

"You didn't give me the opportunity."

"Can we call a truce?" He smiled. "We are working together after all."

She nodded, a slight smile tugging at her lips. "No need to make those around us uncomfortable by causing tension between us."

He reached over and gave her hand a squeeze. "I'm glad."

After dropping the note off at the sheriff's office, he drove them to the supermarket to buy the items on Mrs. White's list. He shoved open his truck door to a brisk wind. A quick glance at the sky showed thickening clouds. "We need to hurry. Looks like snow, maybe sleet."

"Do you get a lot of snow around here?" Mack rushed ahead of him into the store.

"Up on the mountain we do, but not usually until after Christmas. Old-timers predicted back in the summer that we would have a colder than usual winter." He grabbed a shopping cart and headed for the meat department.

"What are you doing?" Mack tilted her head. "You start with dry food, then go to meat and produce. Everyone knows that."

"I don't see why it makes a difference."

"Because things get warm." She shook her head as if he were dense. "Give me the list and follow me with the cart."

"You're bossy." He grinned but followed orders.

He turned down an aisle.

Two men stood at the other end, their harsh glares on Mack.

She slowed, then glanced over her shoulder at Levi. "Romano's men. I recognize them from the alley. They're the ones who stabbed Alex."

"Get beside me, Mack." Next time he left the ranch, he wouldn't leave his gun behind.

For several tense seconds, he and Mack matched the glares of the two men before the men turned and headed down another aisle. Without saying a word, Romano's men had effectively passed on their message. They knew where Mack was and weren't afraid to be out in the open.

Levi didn't see the men again until they left the store and loaded the purchases into the back of the truck. The men leaned against a newer model Ford, arms crossed, eyes trained on Mack. When Levi drove away from the store, the men followed.

"What are they doing?" Mack turned to look out the back window.

"Intimidation, I think." It wouldn't work. Levi had been through a lot worse during his time in the military. A couple of thugs following him did not fill him with dread. They obviously didn't intend harm to Mack. At least not yet.

"It's working. What if they run us off the road? There are several places on the way to the ranch that would send us off the mountain."

"I know this road better than they do." He patted her shoulder. "It'll be okay. Don't let them get to you. It's what they want."

She pulled her coat tighter around her despite the truck heater being on. "It's hard not to."

"I won't let anything happen to you, Mack. I promise."

"What if you can't keep that promise? What if I can't help you stay safe? I failed Alex."

"No, you didn't. You're fighting to bring down the man responsible for his attack. When I make a promise, I keep it." He would not let anything happen to her while he still breathed.

Chapter Seven

When Levi didn't show for breakfast, Mack filled a plate with pancakes and a liberal dousing of syrup and went to the bunkhouse in search of him. She found him hunched over a laptop on a folding table next to a bed.

"What are you doing? I brought you breakfast." She set the plate next to him.

"Wow. Time got away from me. Thanks." He dug into his food like a starving man. "I'm contacting some people I knew during my military police days in hopes of gathering deeper information on Romano."

"Any luck?" She sat next to him. "How do you sleep on this? It's as hard as a rock."

"I like a firm bed. I'm waiting to hear back. If they find something, we'll set up a place to meet."

"Not without me."

He laughed. "Wouldn't dream of it."

His laptop dinged. "Got something." He read the email, then typed a reply. "We're meeting at the diner at eight tonight. My buddy is coming down from St. Louis."

Another late night. Working as a lawyer's paralegal, she'd had plenty. An afternoon nap would give her the energy she'd need. She stood and picked up the empty plate. "I'll meet you on the front porch at seven-thirty?"

"Sounds good." He rubbed his hands together. "We're getting somewhere, Mack."

"Can we trust this guy?"

"Pretty sure we can. He's an informant I've used in the past."

"Informant? Is he a criminal?" She arched a brow.

"Let's say he skirts what is legal. We aren't going to get dirt on Romano by talking to squeaky-clean people, Mack."

"Okay. I trust you." Although she wouldn't trust the informant any further than she could throw him. She carried the plate back to the kitchen and set to work loading the industrial-size dishwasher. Through the window, she could see a team of workers installing a large wrought-iron gate at the entrance. From inside the pantry came the sound of an electric saw cutting through drywall.

"I hope they make this quick." Mrs. White frowned at the piles of food on her usually spotless counter. "It's hard to work with everything out like this."

"Makes it easier to find." Mack smiled, although she agreed. The constant noise over the last hour gave her a headache.

"I'm back." Marilyn sailed into the kitchen, stopped, planted her hands on her hips, and frowned. "What in the world happened while I was gone?"

"Same thing that always happens when a new woman comes to town," Mrs. White said. She smiled at Mack. "No offense. Anyway, the boss is installing a security gate and a panic room. How was your trip with Buster?"

"Relaxing." Marilyn donned an apron. "At least the work is being done before school lets out for Christmas. Otherwise, the twins would be underfoot."

Mack only half listened as the two women discussed plans for Christmas. With Alex missing and with her staying on the ranch, it didn't feel very festive.

"We're going to need a tree. By this time, we've usually already put one up." Mrs. White closed the door to the dishwasher and turned it on. "Dani says this weekend we'll put up all the decorations."

"I'm sure Willy won't mind cutting down a tree," Marilyn said. "I'll ask him when we finish here. Won't feel like the holidays until we have a tree."

"It's cold enough."

Not feeling part of the planning committee, Mack hung up her apron and returned to her tiny house to do some digging online. She found several newspaper articles about Romano being charged with one crime or another, but the man always walked free. Romano found all the loopholes--A t wasn't crossed here, an i wasn't dotted there...hearsay, circumstantial evidence. Nothing ever stuck.

Why? How did he always escape being locked up?

She drummed her fingers on the table. Romano had to have someone higher up on his payroll. Someone that could tamper with evidence. She did a search on the Little Rock police department. Nothing jumped out at her, but there had to be a dirty someone somewhere.

Between investigating and helping with meals, the day flew by for her. At seven-thirty that evening, she waited on the porch for Levi.

"Meeting place has been changed. I've got two informants with information. Since they would attract too much attention in Misty Hollow, we're meeting at a bar in Langley," he said.

"That's a public place, too." Her gaze fell to the gun on his hip.

"According to them, it's a hole in the wall that looks the other way regarding trouble." He opened the passenger side door for her. "We're going to be late."

"Will they wait?"

He nodded. "But not for long."

"What if we're followed like we were coming back from town yesterday?"

"If someone is following us, I'm to drive past and send a text letting them know we'll have to reschedule."

Mack started to feel as if she were in the plot of a thriller novel.

~

A text came through on his phone before they reached Langley. "Read that, please."

Mack grabbed his phone from the console. "The bar is closed for renovations. We're meeting at a Catholic church." She read off the address.

"A shady part of town." He took the next exit off the Interstate. "Stay close." The church wasn't far from the exit.

A light shone through the stained-glass windows. Obviously, this church still held on to the tradition of keeping its doors open for anyone needing to pray after regular hours.

"I'm surprised the priest is okay with a nighttime meeting." Mack pulled her coat tighter around her.

Levi surveyed the parking lot, noted two vehicles parked in the shadows, then opened the door for Mack to enter the building first. Two men sat in a pew halfway to the front. A priest knelt in the front row.

Levi led Mack to the row behind the two men. "Hey, Bill. Dan." Not their real names, and he didn't care. Knowing their real names would've resulted in the three of them getting killed a long time ago.

Once they settled in the pew, the priest stood and slid in beside Mack.

"What's this?" Levi asked, his hand resting on the butt of his gun.

Bill turned. "Don't worry. He knows more than me and Dan combined. Go ahead, Father Murphy."

"First of all, I want to let you know that your brother is fine. He came to me for medical help, and I got him situated in a safe place." The priest's light-colored eyes rested on Mack. "These two men use this church for their…activities quite often."

Levi relaxed. "You know Romano?"

"Yes. He came to me for confession the other day. Said he was on his way to Misty Hollow. They don't have a Catholic church there." He raised a hand when Mack started to talk. "I cannot tell you what he confessed."

"What can you tell us?" If he couldn't speak about the confession, what information could he possibly have?

The priest smiled. "I can tell you what I've heard from the mouths of others while my congregation gathers after the service. They tend to forget I'm here." He leaned forward on his elbows. "Romano has his hand in many pots and uses whatever method will get him what he wants. He isn't opposed to bribery, blackmail, or intimidation. There is speculation that a LRPD officer is on the take. If I were you, I'd watch the mayor of Misty Hollow. The sheriff, too. As the top figures of that town, Romano is certain to reach out to them."

"Not the sheriff." Levi shook his head. "He's ex-FBI and would never go bad." He didn't know the mayor personally.

"I only said to watch them. Romano goes after people of power."

"Folks who oppose them tend to go missing," Bill said. "He has moles in the police force, judges on his payroll, and politicians who owe him favors." He slipped Levi a Jumpdrive. "There're names on here. I'm sure there are others, but this is what we could find."

"Romano is involved in illegal arms deals, money laundering, and human trafficking. I pity Misty Hollow if he sets up base there."

"Why would he?" Levi glanced from one man to the next. "Little Rock has way more opportunities to grow his sordid empire than a small mountain city."

"Because he's greedy," Dan added. "The man is a puppeteer. He is going to do something in Misty Hollow, guaranteed. Miss Anderson might've brought him there, but he'll use it to his advantage."

"Our town has been through trouble like this before. We aren't easily taken down." Levi crossed his arms. "Between the ranch hands and the motorcycle gang, we have plenty of armed citizens who won't hesitate to take down Romano or one of his men if it comes to that."

"That would start a war," Bill said.

"One more reason I should've stayed in Little Rock." Mack hung her head.

"My child, if not you, then who? You, your brother, and Mr. Owens here are our only hope at the moment for bringing this horrible man to justice. You are in Misty Hollow for that very reason." Father Murray patted her back. "God doesn't make mistakes."

"You really think God had my brother stabbed and sent me running to Misty Hollow in some insane plan to bring down Romano?" Her eyes widened.

"No, but He will use the circumstances to bring something good out of it." Father Murphy stood. "Conclude your business here. I'm tired." He returned to the front of the sanctuary.

Levi wanted to get back to the ranch and see what was on the flash drive. He stood and shook hands with Bill and Dan. "I really appreciate the two of you coming down here."

"It benefits all of us to get a man like Romano off the streets." Dan returned his handshake.

"We'll let you know if we find out anything more." Bill nodded, then left through a side door.

"We'd better head back, too." Levi held out his hand for Mack.

She placed hers in his and stood. "Did we find out anything of value? We already knew Romano's a dangerous man."

"I'm pretty sure this Jumpdrive will tell us something." Levi slipped it into his pocket. "Wait here while I make sure it's safe outside."

He opened the door and scanned the area. Bill and Dan waited until they were away from the church before turning on their headlights. Other than that, the area appeared devoid of people. "Come on."

Levi rushed Mack back into the truck and sped to the Interstate. He wouldn't relax until they were back on the ranch. As he kept an eye on the rearview mirror, the tension in his shoulders seemed to ebb the closer they got to safety. He hadn't noticed anyone following them, but letting down his guard could get him and Mack killed. Alex trusted him to keep his sister safe. That's exactly what Levi intended to do.

The new gate loomed at the ranch entrance. "Do you know the code?" Mack asked.

"Nope." He texted Dylan. A few minutes later, they were buzzed through and told the code would be given to everyone in the morning. "I guess I should've told him we were going out."

"Levi, look." Mack drew his attention to the road behind them.

The same truck that had followed them yesterday idled on the other side of the gate. They'd been followed after all.

Chapter Eight

Mack stared at the Christmas tree Willy dragged into the living room after breakfast. "It's massive."

"Biggest one yet." He grinned and wiped his hands on his faded jeans. "Gonna need more ornaments."

"There are quite a few things we need." Dani entered the room. "Mackenzie, would you mind finding Levi and going into town for a few items? I've a list for each of you."

Mack took the two lists. "I don't mind at all. There's no need for Levi to go if he's busy."

"Not only is he our mechanic, but he's also our errand boy." The other woman smiled. "Just don't tell him that."

"It's our secret." Smiling, Mack donned her coat and headed for the garage.

A light snow fell, casting the ranch in an aura of fantasy and silence. She held out her hand to let a snowflake land on the sleeve of her coat, stark against the red wool. When she looked up, Levi smiled at her from the door of the garage.

"You look like a postcard," he said.

Warmth flooded through her. "I love snow. Dani

wants us to head into town and grab some things. We both have a list."

"Let me grab my jacket." He ducked back inside, then came out donned in a denim jacket lined with sheep's wool. "I heard the town is decorated for the holidays now. Main Street will be transformed."

"I can't wait to see it." She loved Christmas. As they drove, she tried to decide what to give Levi. She doubted they'd bring Romano down by then and wanted to be prepared if she spent the holiday on the ranch. Maybe a book. He had liked to read when he was younger. Maybe he still did.

Levi parked at the diner. "Meet you back here at noon for lunch, okay?"

"Sounds great." Buttoning her coat and pulling the collar high on her neck, she headed down the street, admiring the wreaths hanging from lampposts and store doors. Several windows sported Christmas scenes. The bookstore window displayed an animated Santa reading.

A bell jingled as she entered. After locating the new release table, she headed that way and chose several true crime mysteries as a gift for Levi. Then, noting several books she thought the twins might like, she added those to the stack and something for the boss and his wife, plus a cookbook for Mrs. White.

"I should've waited until last for the bookstore." She set her pile on the counter.

"We're offering free gift wrapping," the clerk said. "Why not finish your shopping and pick these up when you're finished?"

"I'll do that, thanks." Outside, her breath mingling with the slow snowfall, she glanced at her list.

Peppermint candy, white chocolate, some pinecones that made the fire change colors—where could she find all of these outside of the supermarket?

Without her car, the supermarket was too far to walk. There. The mercantile and drugstore might have the things she needed.

The back of her neck prickled as if someone was watching her. She glanced over her shoulder. None of the other shoppers paid her more attention than offering a simple "Merry Christmas." She shook off the paranoia and entered the drugstore.

The cashier said the store offered a few items on her list, but informed her she'd find the rest at the mercantile. Noting the time and realizing she only had half an hour to meet up with Levi, she rushed across the street and into the warmth of the mercantile.

For the first time since arriving at the Rocking W, she found herself in the Christmas spirit. Shopping in stores decked out for the holiday did that for her. She handed her list to the portly man behind the counter.

"Yep, I got this. Feel free to browse while I collect them."

"Thank you." She strolled the aisles, amazed at the variety of things from nails to dry food on the shelves. Just like an old-fashioned general store.

Purchases in hand, she stepped back outside and headed in the direction of the diner. Mack had a couple of blocks to go before meeting up with Levi. By the first block, her arms had numbed from the bags she held. She stopped at the entrance to an alley, assaulted by the vision of Alex being stabbed.

A man stepped into view.

Panic surged through Mack as she recognized the

man from the restaurant. She contemplated dropping the bags and running, but she wouldn't get far.

His cold eyes met hers. A predatory smile curled his lips. "You shouldn't have stuck your nose where it didn't belong." He moved forward. "Now, you'll suffer the same fate as your brother."

She dropped the bags and stuck her hand into her coat pocket, her fingers curling around the pocketknife she'd slipped in at the last minute. Would it be enough to save her? She took a step backward, only to find her progress halted.

Levi steadied her, then lunged forward, tackling the man to the ground. The two men struggled filling the air with grunts and the sound of fists hitting fists.

Pulling the knife from her pocket, she held it at the ready in case she needed to help Levi. She'd seen him fight before as a teen, but never with the ferocity he fought with now. He finally landed a solid right punch that knocked the man out cold. Breathing heavily, he turned to Mack.

~

"You okay?" When Levi had seen Mack facing a man who clearly intended her harm, he hadn't given a second thought about rushing to her rescue.

"I'm okay." Tears sprang to her eyes, and she rushed into his arms.

Levi held her close, his heart pounding. The danger wasn't over with him knocking out the man, but holding Mack in his arms made him feel, albeit temporarily, that things would end in their favor. "We need to call the sheriff to come get this man."

She sniffed and took a step back, slipping a knife into her pocket. "Okay."

"Was that a pocketknife?" He arched a brow, a smile spreading across his face.

"It's all I had." She shrugged, then reached for her bags.

"I'll get those. I've already stowed mine in the truck."

"I have more at the bookstore."

"Okay, we'll pick those up, then head to the diner once the sheriff or a deputy arrives." He studied her face, relieved to see the tears had dried. "You're pretty tough, Mackenzie Anderson."

"Not so tough. It's a good thing you were here." She tilted her head. "How did you know I needed you?"

"I didn't. I came looking for you to carry your purchases." He chuckled. "I'm a gentleman like that."

Deputy Hudson and Deputy Shea arrived and cuffed the still unconscious man. "Come to the office later to file a report," Hudson said, grabbing one of the man's arms while Shea took the other one. Together, they hauled him to his feet.

"We'll be there after lunch." Levi's knuckles ached from gripping the handles of the bags.

"Well, I'm very grateful you're a gentleman." The color returned to her face.

At the bookstore, she darted inside, returning with two large bags of gaily wrapped gifts. "Okay. I'm ready to eat."

To keep the wrapped presents out of the weather, he stashed them behind the seats of his truck, then rushed Mack into the diner out of the cold. Inside, he helped her out of her coat, then followed the hostess to a booth by the window.

They both ordered potato soup and bread. Levi

stared at the winter wonderland outside the window as snow continued to fall. "Pretty, but too early in the season to stick around. Most of our snow comes after Christmas."

"I hope it snows on Christmas." Mack smiled. "I was visiting a friend in Arizona once for the holidays, and it was eighty-two degrees on Christmas. Didn't feel natural." Her smile faded. "Those two thugs are across the street watching us."

Levi followed her gaze. "Don't let them intimidate you." He'd told her that before, but after she was almost attacked in the alley, he could understand her fear. Levi almost wished they'd make a move so he could report them to the sheriff. Unfortunately, staring wasn't a crime.

Mack sighed and straightened as their server brought their meal. "The soup is thick and smells delicious."

"Do you want to move tables?"

"If you don't mind."

They carried their bowls and bread to a booth away from the window.

"This is better." Mack settled onto her seat. "I'll enjoy the soup more out of the view of prying eyes. You haven't said anything about the flash drive." She dipped her bread into her soup.

"I haven't been able to get into it yet. There's a code that Bill forgot to give me. I've texted him. In the meanwhile, I keep trying on my own." He spooned the thick cheesy potato soup into his mouth and almost moaned with pleasure.

"Why would he give you the drive and not tell you how to open it?" Mack shook her head. "Are you sure you can trust him?"

"Pretty sure." The code was most likely something easy. Something Bill expected him to know. He'd keep trying until he received a text with the information.

After they finished, Levi drove to the sheriff's office. The snow had quit falling, but the temperature dropped, turning the day frigid.

"We're here to file a report." Levi leaned on the counter and smiled at Doris, the receptionist. "You're looking mighty fine today."

"Go on with you." Her plump cheeks brightened. "You're such a flirt."

"Can't help myself when I'm around you."

"Head on back. The sheriff is in." She grinned and ducked her head.

"I'm starting to feel like this is our second home," Mack said.

"It does feel like it." Levi knocked on the sheriff's door, then ushered Mack ahead of him.

"Glad to see you unharmed, Miss Anderson." The sheriff motioned for them to sit and slid a sheet of paper across his desk. "Fill this out to the best of your ability."

Mack started filling in the blanks.

"Any idea of who he is?" Levi asked.

"He didn't have ID on him, but we picked him out of one of our lineup books. Name is Dick Jones. Has a rap sheet as long as my arm. Petty stuff mostly."

"It didn't seem petty when he approached Mack." Levi crossed his arms. "Does he work for Romano?"

"Most likely, but there's no evidence to support that theory." The sheriff leaned back in his chair. "I doubt he would've killed Miss Anderson. Most likely he would've abducted her and taken her to Romano to find out what she knows."

"Still a felony and mighty scary, but I wouldn't have much to tell him," Mack piped up. "Not yet anyway."

Levi thought about telling the sheriff about the Jumpdrive, but changed his mind. He wanted to know what it held, and he might not get to find out if he turned it over. He'd turn it over once he had a look and take the scolding that would come along with it.

"Here you go." Mack handed the sheet back to Sheriff Westbrook. "It isn't much. We basically stared at each other until Levi arrived."

The sheriff's gaze landed on Levi's scraped knuckles. "Next time, just call the department. If he'd have been armed, you might be dead."

"Sorry. I acted without thinking." Which he'd do again under the same circumstances. He stood and offered a hand to Mack, pulling her to her feet. "We have a truckload of things the boss's wife needs."

"Go on." The sheriff waved a dismissive hand. "I'll contact you if I find out anything else. It's good that one more of Romano's thugs is locked up."

When they returned to the ranch, Levi carried in the bags, leaving the women to sort through everything. Once the decorations came out, he rushed back to the garage before they roped him into stringing lights. Levi had always hated that job ever since his father tasked him with untangling them every year. He'd take a greasy engine over decorating any day.

He'd just rolled under the truck when his phone alerted him to a text message. He rolled back out and snatched the phone from his workbench.

The text contained not only the code to the Jumpdrive, but also the information that Romano was rumored to be at the motel in Langley tomorrow night.

Chapter Nine

Sleet fell, obscuring Mack's view through the front windshield of the truck Levi borrowed from the ranch. He hadn't wanted to use his in case someone recognized it and wondered why she and Levi were parked outside of a motel in Langley. That would raise a lot of questions neither of them wanted to answer.

A light shone through the thin motel curtains. The figure of a man paced back and forth in front of the window. She could only assume the man to be Romano. They hadn't seen him enter the room, but the motel manager told them he was in room six.

"How long do you think we'll have to wait?" She whispered.

"No idea. He might not come out at all."

She groaned and sat back in her seat. A frigid night staked out in front of a seedy motel was not her idea of fun. At least she sat next to Levi. She cut him a sideways glance. His strong profile, chiseled lips. The cute boy had turned into a very handsome man.

The motel room door opened. Mack's heart beat so hard she thought for sure Levi could hear each thump.

Romano exited the room, locked the door, then

sauntered toward a black Mercedes so out of place among the modest sedans and beat-up trucks. He didn't seem to have a care in the world, not glancing around before sliding into the driver's seat.

"Here we go." Levi started the truck, following as Romano headed east in Langley.

"Where's he going?" Mack leaned forward to see through the small clear space in the windshield.

"Looks like he's headed for the industrial section of the city."

"Maybe we'll actually get evidence tonight to put him behind bars."

"That would be nice." He flashed her a quick grin, then sobered. "Don't do anything but copy me, got it?"

She nodded. Stakeouts and tailing a suspect were more up his alley than hers. She was used to retrieving her information from dusty old law books.

Romano pulled onto the cracked asphalt parking lot in front of a vacant warehouse. He got out of his car, slid up a rolling door, then climbed into his car and drove in. A moment later, the door rolled closed.

"Come on." Levi shoved his door open and grabbed binoculars from the dashboard. "We need to get closer. Bring the flashlights."

Mack slung the bag containing things she thought they would need on a stakeout over her shoulder and followed him. They hunkered down behind a rusty dumpster that smelled as if something had died inside it. She wrinkled her nose and tried not to breathe too deeply.

Now that they were closer, the warehouse was easier to see. Weathered metal and cracked concrete, grimy windows where slivers of light flickered through the gaps. Mack shrank back as a semitruck pulled into the parking lot, stopping next to the rolling door.

Three men climbed out of the back and started hauling boxes into the warehouse.

Mack pulled a camera from her bag. "I brought this just in case."

"You're amazing." Levi replaced the binoculars with the camera.

Mack scribbled details into a notebook. Description of the men, the number and approximate size of the boxes, whether they were heavy enough for two to carry or light enough for one. Her breath floated in the chilly night air like wisps of smoke. Despite the gloves she wore, her fingers grew numb, making it difficult to write.

One of the men stopped and stared toward the dumpster as if he knew they were being watched. Levi and Mack froze. Mack's throat tightened.

Levi seemed calm, but the tightness of his jaw and the way his hand rested on the gun holstered at his side told her he was anything but. An eternity passed before the men climbed in the truck and left the warehouse.

As Mack started to unfold her frozen body, a van pulled in. Two men entered the building.

"We need to see inside," Levi whispered.

"How? We'll be spotted." She glanced at the streetlight next to the parking lot. "What if we break the bulb?"

"It'll make too much noise. Besides, the light worked when Romano arrived. He'd be suspicious if it was suddenly shattered." Levi took her hand and stood in a hunched-over position. "We can make it with some luck and speed." The camera in his other hand joined the binoculars that hung from a strap around his neck.

Keeping to a crouch, they darted across the lot as fast as possible. Once they reached the building, Mack plastered her back against the wall and struggled to catch her breath.

"You okay?" Levi asked softly.

"Yes, just breathless." More so now that his gaze fixed on her so intently.

The darkness and the cold seemed to form a bubble around them. She didn't think it possible for her heart to race any faster, but when Levi planted a quick kiss on her lips, she thought the bubble would break free and fly to the heavens.

~

The presence of danger wasn't exactly the most romantic place to kiss, but Mack's pale, frightened face, the slight gasps she made as she tried to catch her breath, and the way she parted her lips…he hadn't been able to help himself—anything to quell her fears.

He shook himself back to sanity and peered sideways through the dirty window to his right.

Romano and two men sat at a folding table next to the unloaded boxes from the semi. None of the boxes were marked to let him know what they held. He pressed closer, straining to hear the men's conversation.

"Are you sure the buyer will be there?" Romano asked. "I don't want to stay in that flea-ridden motel room any longer than necessary. I don't know why you haven't found me a worthy place in Misty Hollow."

"There aren't many vacant houses, Boss," one of the men said. "Those that were vacant were abandoned and falling apart."

"Any for sale?"

"Yep."

"Then buy me one." Romano opened one of the boxes and pulled out a bag. "This ought to cover it." He tossed the bag to the man as Levi snapped a photo.

"One of the boxes holds money. Write that down," he told Mack. They needed to find a way into that warehouse.

The click of her ink pen sounded loud.

He shrank back as the three men headed out of the room. The slam of doors echoed. The rolling door scraped as it opened and closed.

After a few minutes of silence and the men didn't return, Levi sprinted for the door only to find it locked. He moved to the rolling door, grinning as he lifted it just enough for him and Mack to squeeze under.

"What if they come back?" Mack clutched her bag.

"We'll hide." Not that he could see many places big enough other than the piles of boxes. "We need to find out what those men dropped off."

"Hurry. I'll keep watch." She remained near the door while he opened box after box.

Guns, drugs, and money. The guns and drugs he understood, but why would Romano have boxes of cash?

He snapped photos. They had plenty of evidence to take to the sheriff. He carefully closed each box to look as if they hadn't been opened. "Let's get out of here." Levi led Mack at a run to where he'd parked his truck. He didn't breathe easy until they passed the last Langley exit. "So, about that kiss..." He cut a quick glance at Mack.

"Yeah?"

He couldn't see clearly in the dark, but he'd bet her cheeks had turned rosy from more than the cold. "I forgot myself in the heat of the moment. Are you mad?"

"No." She ducked her head. "You surprised me is all."

"Well, you aren't a little girl anymore, Mack. You're a beautiful woman who sometimes takes my breath away and makes me do…things." Levi chuckled and turned his attention back to the road. He sobered knowing he needed to tell her what he'd found on the Jumpdrive. Something that would most likely break her heart.

"Are we going to the sheriff's office?" She asked. "I can text him to meet us there so we can turn over the camera. I don't want those photos in our possession any longer than necessary."

So, she wanted to get back to business. Levi sighed. He could tell her what he'd found when they returned to the ranch. "That's a good idea."

Mack typed the message into her phone. She didn't receive a reply until they reached Misty Hollow. "He says he'll meet us there in ten minutes."

"Perfect." He pulled in front of the sheriff's office a few minutes early.

It didn't take long for Sheriff Westbrook to join them.

Levi rolled down his window. "This is the evidence you need to bring Romano in."

"Good work." The sheriff smiled. "Hope it's worth you getting me out of bed." He took the camera. "If you ever get tired of being a cowboy mechanic, there's a place for you as a deputy."

"I'm happy where I am, but thanks." He'd had enough of law enforcement in the military. If not for Alex and Mack needing his help, he wouldn't be investigating now.

"I'll gather my deputies and head to this warehouse. When we're finished, I'll let you know."

"Thanks." Levi backed away from the building and headed up the mountain.

"Another late night. Mrs. White is going to get tired of me not helping with breakfast." Mack rested her head on the seat.

"It's not bad now that Marilyn is back." How could he bring up the subject of the Jumpdrive? It surprised him that she hadn't asked anymore about what it contained.

He had to wake her when they arrived at the ranch and waited for the gate to open. "We're home."

"Man, I'm tired." She rubbed her eyes. "Can't wait to slip into warm jammies under a thick quilt. I feel frozen to the bone."

The gate fully opened, and he drove through. "Stakeouts aren't much fun in the summer or the winter. You're either sweating or shivering to death." He pulled into the garage and turned off the engine. "There's something I need to tell you before you go." He turned to face her.

"Okay." She tilted her head.

"It's about the Jumpdrive."

"Tell me."

He took a deep breath. "Alex is mentioned several times. It appears he was more involved than he told you."

"How so?" Her eyes widened.

"From what I could tell, Alex was on the payroll as Romano's attorney."

"Impossible." She shook her head. "I would've known."

"You didn't know about the file or the fact he had a girlfriend." He hated the pain he knew he caused her. "It stands to reason that Alex would've hidden other things from you."

"I can't believe it." She shoved her door open and got out. "You must've read it wrong."

"I didn't. I'll send the pertinent files to your email. The rest I have to turn over to the sheriff."

Her eyes flashed. "He'll think Alex is a crook."

"He might be."

Chapter Ten

"Show me what you have." Mack held the door open to her house. "I want to know what's on it before you turn it over."

"You'd better sit down." Levi opened her laptop on the coffee table and inserted the Jumpdrive. After a couple of clicks, an audio file popped up.

Heart in her throat, Mack sat on the sofa next to Levi not sure she wanted to hear what was on the audio. "Okay. Let's do this." She clenched her hands so tight her fingernails stabbed her palms.

"You're positive Romano was behind the hit?" Alex's voice came through the laptop speaker.

"Of course. I was there." Mack didn't recognize the other man's voice. "You aren't going to reveal my identity, are you? That would be signing my death sentence."

"You have my word." The rustle of paper. "I need to know who the next target is. Who is he blackmailing? Locations of the guns. Where does he keep the girls?" Her brother's voice.

"I don't know all that."

"Sure, you do." Alex's voice hardened. "You know everything Romano does."

"You'd better make this worth my time. I'm going to have to leave the country."

Mack shot a glance at Levi. "Who is he talking to?"

"No idea. No names other than Romano's are ever mentioned."

She turned her attention back to the audio.

"I also need to know where he keeps his money."

"That's easy. The Caymans."

Alex sighed. "That's something at least. What about the other issues I mentioned?"

"You're the next target, dude. Not for blackmail or any of his other dealings, but since you turned him down…well, Romano wants you dead."

Mack gasped. Her brother had told her this, she'd seen his attack, but to hear it spoken so coldheartedly sent ice through her veins.

"I'm not as easy to kill as he thinks," Alex said.

"He'll go after your sister if he has to."

Levi gripped Mack's hand. "I won't let that happen. Romano will have to go through me."

"Which he might very well do." How could she keep Levi safe against a man like Romano who had a small army working for him?

"If he touches my sister, I'll kill him myself," Alex said.

"You should never have gotten involved."

"Someone has to bring down his empire."

Mack's feelings clashed. Pride that her brother fought for something so important, fear for the peril he found himself in, and heartbreak over the burden he carried alone. Tears stung her eyes, and she leaned against Levi's solid chest.

"We need to get back into Alex's office," she said. "We've missed something. My brother would have hidden more information than what is on this drive."

"Not until we get some sleep." Levi closed the laptop and stood, helping her to her feet. "Catch what sleep you can. We'll leave in the morning."

"Why not today?" She frowned.

"We won't be any good to anyone without rest. Plus, I need to get this drive to the sheriff today. It's too important to hold onto."

She shrugged. "We don't know the identity of the man he spoke with. How is that going to help the sheriff?"

His expression softened. "There's more on there. He spoke to a few other men. I've copied the recording and will show it to you after you've slept."

"I'd rather hear it all now."

"Sleep, sweetheart." He planted a tender kiss on her forehead. "Come get me when you wake up."

"We really need to find Alex."

"I'm working on it." He gave her a soft smile, then left, closing her door behind him.

Mack locked the door and headed upstairs to the loft and her bed. She lay and stared at the wooden beams across the ceiling, doubting sleep would come. Poor Alex. He'd gotten himself into something so deep and evil that he might not find his way out. Something that would be coming for Mack next.

Rolling onto her side, she hugged her extra pillow to her chest. Thank God for Levi. At least Mack wasn't alone in taking up where her brother had left off. She would have a hand in bringing Romano to his knees and making sure the man spent the rest of his life behind bars.

At some point, her mind stopped whirling, and she slept. When she woke, her stomach growled, letting her know she'd missed not only breakfast, but lunch as well. She yawned, stretched, and padded downstairs, pleased to see someone had left her a sandwich and chips on her small dining table. She took the sandwich with her in search of Levi.

Mack found him in the bunkhouse, his hair wet from a recent shower. "Thanks for the sandwich."

He rubbed a towel over his hair. "I didn't leave it. Must have been Mrs. White who left it. Did you want to go with me to drop off the Jumpdrive?"

"Absolutely. We do everything that pertains to this case together."

~

They left for Little Rock again at seven the next morning. Levi almost mentioned they should stay in the city until Romano was brought to justice, but knowing the man's thugs were in Misty Hollow made him change his mind. In order not to keep going back and forth, they needed to find Alex's notes this time around.

"I'm sorry your work has been set on the back burner." Mack placed a hand on his arm.

"It's okay. The vehicles aren't going anywhere." He smiled, patting her hand. "I want to help you and Alex."

"You don't regret me coming to the ranch?"

"Not for a minute." He raised her hand to his lips, then took the exit that led to Alex's office. "What do we do about the receptionist?"

"Tell her the truth. That we're there to pick up

some files for a case I'm working on." Her cheeks turned pink as she slipped her hand free.

Inside Alex's office, relieved not to see Sarah at her desk, Levi headed for the bookshelves while Mack sat again at her brother's desk. He half expected one of the books would reveal a hidden safe when moved. Disappointment flooded through him when they didn't.

"Can I help you look for something?" Sarah stood in the doorway, a questioning look on her face.

"No, we're fine," Mack said. "I just forgot something when we were here the other day."

"What is it? I could've mailed it to you." Her eyes darted from Levi to Mack.

"That's okay." Mack grinned. "How about some coffee?"

"Sure." With a wary glance at the two of them, she turned and left.

"I thought you told her not to come in for a while?" Levi frowned.

"I did." Mack stared after her, then returned to the desk. She thrust her arm into a deep drawer up to the elbow.

A loud click sounded. "Bingo." Her grin widened. "I knew Alex had to have another hiding place in this big desk." She pulled out a large binder, keeping it below the desk as Sarah returned with the coffee. "I can't find the file on Mr. Williams. Do you know where it is?"

"I have it on my desk to make copies. I'll get right on that." Relief flooded Sarah's face.

"After that, take some time off. I mean it. If I find you here again, I'll change the locks." The determined glint in Mack's eyes belied her smile.

Sarah faltered. "Okay. It's just...uh...I don't know what to do with myself."

"Take a vacation." Mack kept a smile in place until the woman left. "I don't need the file on Williams, but it got her out of our hair."

"I didn't think you did." He laughed. "Give me that binder. I'll stick it in my coat, and we'll go through it at supper. I know a nice burger joint that's out of the way."

"Sounds wonderful." She handed him the binder and closed up the desk, taking the files she didn't need from Sarah on their way out of the office.

Doing his best to make sure they weren't being followed, Levi drove to the burger place he'd mentioned. A small mom-and-pop diner that most people wouldn't give a second glance to unless they'd had the privilege of having eaten there. "You won't find a better burger in the whole state," he said, opening the door for Mack.

He requested a back corner booth, then followed the hostess. She handed them menus with promises to return. "Want to wait until we eat to go through this?" He set the binder on the table.

"Yes. I'm actually starving. If this gives us what we need, we won't need to come back until this is all over."

She wouldn't need to come back. Knowing she'd leave Misty Hollow once Romano was behind bars clenched his heart in an icy grip. Seeing her every day, spending time with her—it had all become a routine he looked forward to when he woke. The thought of her leaving filled him with sadness. He'd let too much time pass since seeing his best friend and his little sister.

Not so little anymore. Mack had grown into a beautiful woman—one he wanted to get to know better. What dreams did she hold? What was her favorite color? Did she want to marry and have a family or was she married to her career?

They both ordered mushroom Swiss burgers with fries and soda. Once the server left, Levi opened the binder and spread the pages across the table.

Among the documents in front of them were a list of names, dates, and locations linked to Romano's criminal network. Levi recognized a few of the names from the news. He spotted offshore bank-account numbers, dates of meetings, even a sketch of Romano's organizational hierarchy.

"Do you realize what we have here?" Mack's eyes widened. "We have everything we need to lock Romano up."

"Alex had been working on this for a long time. He had to have been before Romano came to him with the job offer." Most of the pages had what Levi assumed were notes written in Alex's handwriting underlining key details and connecting different pieces of information with arrows and notes such as "cross-check M's alibi" or "possible mole."

"He could've found out so much more by agreeing to work with Romano while taking down these notes. How did he obtain all this info?"

"He must have an informant. We need to find out who that informant is."

"His girlfriend?"

"Maybe." Levi crossed his arms. It sure wouldn't hurt to question Rebecca Miller again. She'd gone to meet up with Romano quick enough.

"They could've been working together." Mack dipped a fry into ketchup. "Have you heard from the sheriff after dropping off the drive?"

"Not yet. He's going to love all this."

"We should make copies first."

"Agreed." He shoved all the evidence back into the binder.

"What's wrong?" She tilted her head. "Aren't you excited about what we found? This is what we need."

"Of course, I am. But, if someone finds out we have this information and that we've read through it, they'll be coming for us. Same as they did for Alex."

The target on their backs had grown by ten sizes.

Chapter Eleven

Outside, the wind rattled the loose boards, causing Mack's tiny house to creak. It was as if the wind penetrated the walls to drag her into the open where danger lurked.

After a night of nightmares where Romano had come for her, Mack had opened the door the next morning to an anxious Levi. He'd plopped his laptop on the table and told her he'd received an encrypted signal telling him to be ready at eight a.m.

Now, cups of coffee in hand at three minutes before eight, the two of them stared at a blank screen. At exactly the appointed time, Rebecca Miller's face appeared on the screen. Her once vibrant features were now marked by exhaustion and fear, her lips pressed into a thin line that quivered as she spoke. Dark shadows alluded to nights of little sleep.

"Thank you for talking with me," she said, glancing over her shoulder. "I have some information you should have. Now's not the time. Can we meet?"

Mack shot Levi a sharp look. "Can we trust her?" she whispered.

"We have to." He turned back to the screen. "When and where?"

"I'm in Misty Hollow. There's an old barn on Highway 105. You'll recognize it by all the woodpecker holes. Turn by the mailbox that looks like a rooster. Meet me at ten p.m. Make sure you aren't followed."

"Do you have any information on my brother?" Mack leaned in so Rebecca could see her.

"I'm afraid not." Tears shimmered in the other woman's eyes. "I fear he's dead. No one has mentioned his attack. It's as if he's never had dealings with Romano. I need to go. See you later." The screen went dark.

Mack stared at the laptop. "What if it's a trap?"

"What if it isn't?" Levi closed the computer. "It's a chance we have to take."

"What did the sheriff say about the files?"

"That it would take time for him to go through them." He picked up his coffee mug from the table.

At the best of times, Mack wasn't a patient woman. Less so now that there was so much at stake. One day of rest, and another late night loomed in front of them. Not to mention winter had arrived with a vengeance.

The day dragged with mundane chores in the house. After supper, Mack didn't think she'd ever conquer the mound of dirty dishes. When she finally did, she hurried back to her house and pulled out the warmest clothes she'd brought with her, which wasn't much. She hadn't planned on staying more than a day or two.

Over all the tasks of the day hung Rebecca's words about Alex being dead. Mack refused to believe so without a body. Yes, Romano probably had many ways to dispose of a body where it wouldn't be found, but until she had proof her brother no longer walked the earth, she hung onto hope she'd see him again.

At nine p.m., she dressed in warm layers and met Levi in front of the house. Christmas lights twinkled from where they were strung on the front porch eave. Despite the festive decorations, it didn't feel like Christmas.

They rode in silence until Mack spotted a leaning mailbox with a wooden rooster perched on top. Levi turned down a rut-filled dirt road.

One pothole caused Mack to bounce off her seat and her teeth to clatter. "At least it looks as if we won't be found. No one goes down this road." She gripped the handle to the right of her head.

"Let's hope it doesn't rattle my truck into pieces." Levi slowed the vehicle to a walking pace. "I wouldn't want to have to wait for a tow truck in this cold."

Mack peered through the dark as they approached a barn so full of holes the moon shown through the walls, that she didn't see how it still stood. Now it leaned like a forgotten sentinel in a weed-grown field. The moonlight did nothing to dispel its menacing silhouette, although it might look quaint in the daylight.

Debris littered the ground—rusty farm tools, shards of glass from shattered windows, and remnants of what might once have been a thriving farm. The frigid air was thick with the smell of damp earth and decaying wood.

Like shadows, Levi and Mack skirted the perimeter, then inched into the barn. Every whistle of the wind through the woodpecker holes tensed Mack's muscles. Using hand signals, Levi motioned for her to go one way while he went the other. Rebecca wasn't expected for another fifteen minutes.

After determining they were alone, Mack yanked an axe out of a stump then used the stump to sit on. She tucked her hands into her armpits in a vain attempt to get warm.

Levi stood behind her and wrapped his arms around her. "Hopefully, this won't take long."

"If it does, we'll freeze." She shivered so hard her chin quivered. The temperature almost made her forget why they'd come. Almost.

"When she gets here, I want you to duck into one of these stalls. Stay out of sight until we know whether she can be trusted. If she's brought Romano or his men, at least they won't get both of us."

"What?" She glanced back. "I'm not leaving you." She'd done that to Alex. Never again would she flee.

"There'll be no justice for Alex if we both perish."

"Fine." Footsteps outside sent her darting into a stall.

~

Levi stiffened as Rebecca entered the barn. The dim light of the moon revealed how frail she'd become. The dark coat she wore hung on her frame. Despite the fear etched on her face, determination shone in her eyes.

She fished something from her pocket, then handed him a flash drive. Her hand shook as she dropped it into his outstretched palm. "You may know some of this already if you've located Alex's files, but what you don't know is the identity of Romano's next target."

"Who is it?" He pocketed the drive.

"The new mayor of Misty Hollow."

Mayor Hilton? "Why? He's only been mayor for a few months." Misty Hollow went through mayors like children did candy. Mostly because the mayors had been corrupt.

"Because he won't follow orders." She shrugged. "Your city has finally voted in someone with a conscience. Hilton, if pressured enough by authorities, may remember some things Romano would rather he didn't."

"Like what?" He frowned.

"All the things on that drive."

"Stop being evasive. What does the mayor know that can get him killed, and why hasn't he said something before now?"

She glanced around the barn, clearly wanting to make a quick getaway. "He knows which politicians have their hand in Romano's organization. Photos on that drive reveal them at a party Romano gave last New Year's Eve. A party where he supplied young girls. Rumor has it, Hilton fled as soon as he realized what was happening."

"Why hasn't he come forward with this information?" Levi wouldn't have hesitated.

"He has a family. You know what Romano would do to them if Hilton talked."

"Is he going after them too?" Levi needed to get a hold of Sheriff Westbrook ASAP. "When is this happening?"

"No mention of that at this time. The hit is scheduled to happen soon. I'd say within the next day or two. Before Christmas for sure. I have to go. Be careful. There's already talk of your and Mackenzie's investigating." She gripped his arms. "Please let me know if you hear from Alex."

"Absolutely." They wouldn't hear from him. Levi feared the worst.

With a nod, Rebecca whirled and fled back into the night.

Mack exited the stall she'd taken cover in. "We have to let Hilton know."

"We'll visit the sheriff first thing in the morning."

She clutched his sleeve. "Now, Levi. We'll go to his house. A man's life, possibly his family's life, is at stake."

"Okay. I also want to get a look at the photo on this drive."

"We can do that in the truck. I brought my laptop."

They rushed back to the truck where Levi cranked the heater on high. He inserted the drive into the laptop and scrolled through files he'd already seen until he reached the file marked Photos.

He recognized the LRPD chief of police, the former mayor of Misty Hollow, Romano, another small-town mayor—all with young pretty girls beside them as they posed with Romano. The girls were clearly underage.

"This is huge, Levi." Excitement laced Mack's words. "This is enough to bring down his organization even without the guns and the cash. Best of all, we'll save those girls."

This was the beginning of something much larger and more dangerous than he had anticipated. Not only would Romano want to stop him and Mack, but the other men at the party would also.

They bounced their way back to the highway and sped up the mountain to the sheriff's house. Other than a light on the porch and Christmas lights hanging from the eaves and draped over bushes, no lights shone in the house.

"Don't worry. This is too big for him to be upset about being awakened." Mack shoved her door open and raced for the porch.

By the time Levi joined her, she'd already banged on the door.

The sheriff, clad only in plain pajama bottoms yanked open the door, his hand clutching a revolver. "What happened?"

Mack pushed her way inside. "It's too cold to stay out there." She rattled off the details about the meeting with Rebecca Miller.

The sheriff's face darkened as he listened. "You should've had a couple of deputies with you. This is getting too dangerous for the two of you to keep investigating on your own."

"Here's the drive." Levi handed it over. "The only thing new are the photos." He chose to disregard the sheriff's statement about deputies. If Rebecca had spotted anyone but him or Mack, she wouldn't have shown up, and they wouldn't know about the upcoming assassination.

Mack planted her fists on her hips. "Instead of a lecture, you should thank us. You can quite possibly save a man's life now."

The sheriff's shoulders relaxed. "Thank you, but, I stand by my statement on the danger. It's time for the two of you take a few steps back."

"Wouldn't help anything." Levi shook his head. "Romano probably already knows we've got the files. If he doesn't, he suspects we're close. Targets are already affixed to our backs." Great big red ones.

"You two go home. I need to set something in place to protect the Hilton family. Come, Shadow." He motioned for the black German shepherd who had been quietly watching them from the living room, then escorted Mack and Levi to the door, locking it behind them.

Back in the truck, Levi released a heavy sigh. "It's been quite the few days."

"Yes. Other than finding Alex, our work might be finished."

"What then?" He faced her. "You going to return to Little Rock?"

"Not yet." Her gaze searched his. "It's too dangerous for me to go back. Unless you want me to?"

"I most certainly do not." He smiled, relieved she'd be sticking around for a while. "Maybe we can actually enjoy the Christmas holiday now."

"Maybe." She smiled and clicked her seatbelt into place. "It won't be the same without Alex, but if we get Romano locked up by Christmas, my brother will come out of hiding."

He wanted to tell her not to hold too tight to the hope Alex was alive, but he didn't have the heart. What did it hurt to allow her a bit of hope?

Unless he gained the gift of seeing the future, he'd keep his mouth shut. If Alex was alive, he'd show up. If he wasn't, time would pass, and Mack would have to accept the heartbreaking news.

Chapter Twelve

Mack's patience thinned when it took three days of waiting for the sheriff to get back to them on the files they'd given him as well as three days of hearing nothing from Romano.

Mack pressed the button on the microwave to soften the butter for the breakfast biscuits. Over it all hung the worry of what she should do once Romano was out of the picture. If her brother was still alive, her life could return to normal. She'd go back to work, satisfied she'd avenged his attack.

If her brother was found dead…she didn't want to think on that possibility. She'd have to close the law business since she didn't have a law degree.

Then, there was Levi. Could she leave him in her rearview mirror? Her childish crush on her brother's friend had turned into so much more. She didn't know if she was strong enough to walk away from him.

She scowled through the kitchen door at the Christmas tree that twinkled in the dining room. Every room downstairs had a tree. She normally loved Christmas, but not this year. Not without her brother.

Of course, Christmas was more than decorations and missing family members, but those things had always been a big part of the holidays for her. Now, she'd spend the holiday among strangers. Not counting Levi, of course.

Butter softened, she set it on the dining room table as Marilyn rang the cowbell out front. Through the large window, lazy snowflakes drifted down. The snow came early this year, according to Mrs. White, but the woman also said it wouldn't stick.

Mack tore her gaze away from the idyllic view and returned to the kitchen for the biscuits hot from the oven while the other two women carried in platters of scrambled eggs and bacon.

Levi trailed his fingers across her back as he took his seat. "Felt good to get a few nights of good sleep."

"Hmm." She'd tossed and turned most the night worrying about Alex.

Her phone dinged signally a text. She glanced at the screen. Sarah. She'd call her back later. The woman was supposed to be on vacation.

After breakfast was finished and the dishes done, Mack read the text from Sarah.

Got a message on office phone. Said if you want news on Alex to go to this address in Langley at nine p.m. tonight. No cops.

Mack immediately went in search of Levi who was cleaning engine parts in the garage. The scent of oil and grease hung heavy in the air. She showed him the text.

"No mention of who left the message." He frowned. "It could be a trap."

"Could be, but we still have to go. We can't let

any opportunity to find Alex pass."

He handed her back the phone. "I agree. We'll be there, but expect anything. Meet me at my truck at eight-twenty."

Wearing her warmest clothes, Mack waited by Levi's truck at eight-fifteen. He grinned as he joined her. "Prompt as usual."

"Anxious, excited—you name it. We might finally find out something about Alex." She slid into the truck and clicked her seatbelt into place. "Did you bring your gun?"

"Absolutely. You should carry a weapon, you know."

"I've got pepper spray and a Taser. Had them for years and never needed them."

"Start carrying them with you." He backed from the house and sped down the mountain.

Half an hour later, they pulled into a parking lot of an abandoned building. The place was part of an industrial park. All the buildings resembled ghosts showing very little of what they once were.

Sarah stepped from the shadows.

"What is she doing here?" Mack wanted to strangle the woman. "Does she have any sense at all?" She shoved her door open and marched toward her receptionist. "Why are you here?"

"I want to know what happened to Alex, same as you." Her eyes glittered in the moonlight.

"You have no idea the danger you've put yourself in." Mack glared.

"There's nothing we can do about her now." Levi put a hand on the small of Mack's back. "It's bitterly cold tonight. Let's get this over with."

"Follow me. I came early and scoured the place. Think I know where the meeting might be held," Sarah said. "There's a smaller building in the center of the compound. Fresh footprints in the dusting of snow on the ground."

Mack glanced at Levi who shrugged, then back at Sarah. "Okay. Lead the way." Mack's skin prickled with tension. Sarah had always professed wanting to pursue a law degree or become a paralegal like Mack, but leading them to a potential meeting with an informant, one of Romano's men, or Romano himself was a very foolish move.

Sarah led them through the dimly lit industrial buildings. A clatter from her right made Mack jump. She gave a sigh of relief as a stray cat emerged from behind a battered metal trash can.

As they moved cautiously among the vacant buildings, Mack studied the ground around them. No footprints other than what she surmised to be Sarah's. Where were the prints of the person they were going to meet? Was there another way in and out of the industrial park?

Were they walking into a trap? Mack pulled her coat tighter around her.

Sarah didn't seem nervous in the slightest. She strode ahead of them, head up, back straight, not once glancing back to make sure they followed.

Mack didn't like it. Not a bit. Her steps faltered and she hung back. "Something isn't right," she whispered.

~

"I agree." Levi gripped her hand. "Stay close. Head for that space between those two buildings when I say. Race through it, then head to where we left the truck."

Eyes wide, she nodded.

Two men stepped around the corner of a building, guns in hand.

"Go!" Levi gave Mack a shove as the first shot rang out. Another sounded as he darted into the space he'd ordered Mack to go.

He spared a backward glance to see Sarah speaking with the two men. After several terse words he couldn't understand, Sarah continued in the direction she'd been leading them. It had been a trap. Mack's receptionist knew the men.

Not knowing the park, Levi felt at a definite disadvantage. It would be easy to run in circles in the unfamiliar area.

Mack stopped ahead of him.

"I don't know which way." Her voice shook.

He glanced at the sky in hopes of getting his bearings. Heavy cloud cover hid the moon. He turned right. "This way." He hoped. A fine sleet began to fall. If they didn't find their way out soon, they'd have to take cover against the frigid cold. The last thing he wanted was to spend time in a concrete building in a sleet storm with armed men chasing them.

When a curse reached his ears, he spurred Mack faster. Think, man.

Finding their way out would've been a lot easier if Sarah hadn't led them in a zigzag. Had that been on purpose?

A scream echoed. Then another gunshot from a different direction. If there were two or more groups, he and Mack would be boxed in with no way to escape. He pulled his cell phone from his pocket to call for help. No service.

The trap had been well-thought-out. Lure them into a maze of two-story buildings with no cell service.

The murmur of voices alerted him their pursuers were getting closer. Levi pushed open the nearest door and yanked Mack in after him. Closing the door as softly as he could, he led her to the back of the room and ducked behind some empty copy paper boxes. Not much of a shield, but he hoped the men would go on by.

Through the grimy window, he made out their shapes.

"They have to be here somewhere," one of them said. "If we return without getting rid of them, it'll be our heads."

"They won't get away." The other man cursed. "Start searching the buildings. They won't be in this one. She's in there."

"So?"

"No one is going to stay in a dark room with a dead body. Use your head."

The men moved on.

"Dead body?" Mack's whisper rose.

"Shh." Did he dare risk a light? He waited several terse minutes, then pulled a small flashlight from his pocket, shining it around the room.

A few feet away lay Rebecca Miller, a bullet between her wide eyes.

Mack gasped. "They discovered she was trying to bring Romano down."

"Shh." Despite knowing the woman couldn't have survived the gunshot, Levi checked for a pulse anyway. Nothing. "Come on. We can't stay here." They needed to let law enforcement know where to find Rebecca.

He led Mack through another door. The clouds parted, allowing him to get his bearings. "Run and don't look back. That way." He pointed to where the truck was.

"Where are you going to be?"

"Right beside you."

Throwing caution to the sleet and wind, they raced toward the truck, the pounding of their feet loud on the concrete. They yanked the doors to the truck open and climbed inside. Mack backed up, spun around, and sped away from the area before buckling his seatbelt.

"Will they follow?" Mack stared out the back window.

"I doubt it. They know where to find us." They couldn't trust anyone other than the sheriff's department and those on the ranch.

"I can't believe Sarah tried to turn us over to Romano." Mack shook her head.

"You've never seen any deception from her before?"

"No. It explains why she was always at the office late. I bet she was looking for the files we found so she could hand them to Romano."

"That's my guess as well. See if you can get a hold of the police to let them know where to find Rebecca's body."

"Alex is going to be so upset." She pressed buttons on her phone. When someone answered, she rattled off the address of the industrial park and mentioned they could check their credentials with the Misty Hollow sheriff's department. "You're not going to believe this. The guy on the phone threatened to press charges because we fled the scene of a crime. Did he want us to get killed?"

"The officer doesn't know us. Don't take it personal." He reached for her hand. "You did great back there."

"I was terrified. I didn't think we were going to make it out."

"But, we did."

"Thanks to your quick thinking." She leaned against the back of her seat. "We still don't know anything about the whereabouts of Alex."

"Maybe not, but Romano is starting to make mistakes. That means he's getting worried. We're getting close."

"You really think so? I feel like we're spinning our wheels."

He gave her hand a squeeze. "Don't lose hope. We have enough information to put him away for good. All we have to do is find him."

"In Misty Hollow."

"Yes." A place full of hunting cabins and woods. Misty Mountain held a hundred places for someone to hide out. A man like Romano could purchase a secluded house somewhere and hole up, making locating him difficult. But, he'd have to come out sometime. When he did, they'd get him—hopefully without anyone else getting hurt. Tonight, he and Mack had been too close to being killed. He couldn't let that happen again. If he could lock her up on the ranch to keep her safe, he would.

Mack's fingers flew across her phone's keyboard. "I'm filling the sheriff in on our night."

"Good idea." He rounded the last hairpin curve before reaching the turnoff to the ranch.

An unfamiliar car idled in front of the gate. Two armed men leaned against the vehicle, seemingly oblivious to the night's chill. When they spotted Levi's truck, they opened fire.

Chapter Thirteen

Riding hell-bent for leather came the Rocking W ranch hands on horseback. Mack had never understood the old saying, but she was mighty glad they were here. She stared through the front windshield as Romano's men whipped around to face the arriving posse.

"Get down!" Levi's voice cut through the tension like a whip as he shoved Mack's head to her knees.

Bullets whizzed overhead, shattering glass and pinging the truck's body.

"We have to help." Mack fought against his hold. She wasn't one to back down, not even in the face of danger.

"They don't need our help. What we have to do is stay alive." He spun the truck around and sped up the mountain, away from the ranch and the place she'd started to feel safe.

Fire burned through her upper left arm. "I'm hit."

Levi shot her a glance. "How bad?"

"I don't know." Couldn't be that bad, right? She still sat in the seat rather than slumped over. "Where are we going?"

"Deep into the woods." He yanked the steering

wheel to the right and down a worn dirt road before veering off again. Each turn he took had them on a rougher and rougher road. A bitter wind blew through the broken windows.

Levi's lips moved silently despite the tension radiating from him.

"Are you praying?" Mack widened her eyes.

"Seems like a good time to do so, don't you think?" He veered onto yet another path that could barely be called a road until they arrived at a cabin.

"This is a hunting cabin?" Mack's mouth fell open.

A two-story A-frame with a wraparound porch stood like a sentinel in a cleared portion of the mountain. A stone chimney rose on one side.

"It's a vacation home."

"Yours?" She arched a brow.

"Hardly. Belongs to the sheriff's mother-in-law." He chuckled and faced her, then his smile vanished. "Where are you hit?"

"My arm." She gently pushed her finger through the hole in her coat and winced. "I don't think it's bad."

"Let's go inside so I can take a look." He shoved his door open, then circled to help her out.

"Your poor truck." Bullet holes riddled the door panel on the passenger side. It was a wonder she hadn't been killed. Knowing how close they'd come to meet their maker, her knees buckled.

Levi scooped her into his arms and set her on a wicker chair on the porch before lifting a gnome from a flowerpot and removing a key. At her questioning look, he said, "We've all used the cabin now and then. I'm the first to need it as a hideout, though." He unlocked the door and helped her inside and onto a kitchen chair. "Stay put. I'm going to take a quick look around and locate a first aid kit."

"Okay." She glanced around the wood-paneled cabin. Rustic and modern. A very comfortable place for them to spend some time. "Is there any way we can get someone to bring our notes and laptops to us?"

"I'll check," he called from the other room. "We have to make sure no one can get to us until we're safely back on the ranch."

She agreed. Seeing how quickly the other cowboys had rushed to confront the danger, she couldn't think of a better place to be while Romano walked free.

Levi returned and set a first aid kit on the table. "Let me start a fire. Can you take your coat off?"

"I think so." It wasn't easy, but she eventually slipped her arm free.

Levi soon had a fire roaring in the fireplace.

Taking the first aid kit in her good hand, Mack moved to the sofa, closer to the warmth of the flames. "I think it's just a graze." She showed him where blood soaked through the sleeve of her sweater.

"Can you take off your shirt?"

Her mouth opened and closed like a fish. "Aren't you going to at least buy me dinner first?"

"What?" He frowned. "Oh." His face reddened. "I'm used to the guys. I'll just cut off the sleeve."

"I'm teasing you. I'm wearing a tank top underneath, but I will need your help."

He rushed to help ease the sweater over her head, then cleared his throat and opened the first aid kit. "You're right. Just a graze."

She stared at the red gash across her arm. Her stomach roiled. "I don't do blood very well."

His eyes widened. "You aren't going to pass out, are you? Here. Lie down." He helped her onto her back. As he gazed down at her, his eyes darkened. He smoothed a stray lock of hair from her face, then dropped his gaze to her lips.

The air between them crackled. The pain in her arm ebbed.

"I could've lost you today," he said softly.

"I'm still here." Thanks to his quick thinking.

"Ah, to hell with it." He cupped her face and kissed her.

Her breath fled as his kiss deepened. Maybe it wasn't a good idea for the two of them to be alone.

Levi pulled back and rested his forehead against hers. "I owe Alex a debt of gratitude."

"Why?" She asked, her voice hoarse.

"For bringing you back into my life." He straightened and reached for an antiseptic cleaning pad. "This might sting."

She winced as he dabbed at her wound, then smeared some antibacterial ointment on it before applying a bandage. "Looks like I'll live."

"The bedrooms are upstairs. Can you make it?" He put the medical supplies away.

"Yes. How long do you think we'll have to stay here?"

"I'm hoping only until morning. The other ranch hands will come for us." He stood and held out his hand. "There are worse places to have to hide."

~

Levi lay in bed and stared at the ceiling. He hoped

help would come. They couldn't stay hidden forever. Romano's men would search the woods and would eventually find the cabin. For now they were safe.

His mind drifted back to the kiss. Maybe it hadn't been the right time, but seeing her lying there as he leaned over her…he hadn't been able to help himself. He shouldn't be having romantic ideas at a time like this. Not until Romano was locked up and Alex was found. He and Mack both needed to keep their wits about them. Every rustle of a tree branch outside put him on high alert. Sleep was a long time coming.

In the morning, he headed down the stairs to the aroma of brewing coffee and Mack, her arm in a makeshift sling, standing at the sink. "Should you be doing anything?"

"Why not?" She shrugged. "I've got one good arm, and I found some coffee."

"Great, thanks." He took a cup then searched drawers and cupboards for a radio. With poor cell phone service, most mountain cabins had one. He located it in the cupboard above the refrigerator. After replacing the batteries, he called the ranch.

"That you, Levi?" Dylan's voice came through.

"Yes. We're at Sheriff Westbrook's mother-in-law's cabin. Is everyone there okay?"

"Yes. We successfully ran off the threat."

"Is there a back way to the ranch? We can't stay here."

"There is, but you'll have to walk part of the way." Dylan rattled off directions. "Keep the radio with you. I'll send some hands to meet up with you. Be careful." He clicked off.

Levi turned to Mack. "You up to a long hike?"

"It's my arm that's injured, not my legs. I'll do what needs doing." She washed her cup and set it on the drainboard.

He drank his as fast as he could without burning his mouth, then helped Mack into her coat and gloves. Outside, the air smelled strongly of pine. Their breath hung in the cold air. His truck would do little to protect them from the weather. At least it didn't look like snow.

Following the directions Dylan had given him, Levi drove as far as the truck could go. "We walk from here."

"How far is it?"

"A couple of hours." He sighed. Levi took Mack's hand and led her through the forest. Every rustle of a leaf or snap of a twig raised the hair on his neck, despite knowing Romano's men couldn't have tracked them yet. They still had some time. "Stay close. I don't think we're being followed yet, but we can't afford to make any noise. If they spot us, we split up."

"Absolutely not."

He stopped and turned her to face him. "Yes. I'll lead them away from you. Once Alex is found, he'll need you."

"You're his best friend."

"You're his sister." He wouldn't be deterred.

The rumble of a far-off engine alerted him that his truck had been found much sooner than he'd hoped. He gripped Mack's hand again. "We've got to move faster." Where was the help Dylan had promised them?

After what seemed like an eternity, they reached a ridge that overlooked the ranch. From their vantage point, they could see the ranch hands and horses milling around. The horses wouldn't be able to make it up the ridge. It was up to Levi and Mack to find a way down.

He turned left, moving as quickly and quietly as possible through the thick underbrush. They found a path that led steadily downward. It wouldn't be easy. "Hold on to me. It's going to be slippery."

The occasional gasp or whimper escaped her, sending regret straight through his heart at how the path they had to take caused her pain. He slipped his arm around her waist in a vain attempt to make the trek easier for her.

"We're going too slow," she said, glancing behind them. "They're going to catch up. You need to leave me and go for help."

"No."

"You said we might have to split up. Now is the time."

"I've changed my mind." He tightened his hold on her.

The crash of brush behind them spurred them to step up their pace. Romano's men weren't trying to be quiet. Why should they? They weren't the ones being hunted.

Maybe he and Mack should find a place to hide until the men passed. Levi had a weapon. He could lay an ambush. Levi glanced at Mack's pale face. No. He couldn't risk her getting caught in the crossfire. They needed to keep going until the ranch hands caught up with them.

The rustle of bushes behind them grew louder. Ahead of them came the sounds of hooves on packed dirt. Mack and Levi were about to be caught in the middle of a gunfight.

The ranch hands came into sight the same time

Romano's men did.

Levi shoved Mack into the brush and dove after her as the first gunshot rang out. Shielding her body with his, he expected to feel the impact of a bullet at any moment.

Mack lay still under him, her body trembling. He pressed closer, trying to share his body warmth and comfort.

His ears rang by the time the shooting stopped. He lifted his head to see River grinning down at him.

"Good thing we didn't need you to help us shoot." The other man reached down and helped Levi to his feet.

"I had other things to do." He helped Mack stand.

"I see that." River frowned. "She injured?"

"A graze from the fight at the gate last night." Levi glanced over to where the two Romano men lay unmoving. "They dead?"

"Yep. We'll call the sheriff's department to come take care of the bodies. Our priority is getting the two of you to the warmth of the ranch." River led them to a horse.

With Mack in the saddle in front of him, Levi took one more glimpse of the two dead men. Romano would exact revenge. Of that Levi was certain.

Chapter Fourteen

"Those were two of my best men." Romano punched a hole in the wall, hating being stuck in this hillbilly town. He craved the nightlife, but he needed to keep an eye on his business. But now, some stupid lawyer and his sister had messed everything up. The dead men they'd killed not only worked for him; they were family—nephews.

"They were outnumbered, sir," the bearer of bad news said.

"Where are the cowboy and the woman now?" Romano growled, planting his hands flat on the tabletop in front of him.

"On the ranch. There's no way in without being spotted."

Romano fell back into a chair. He needed to come up with a plan to lure the cowboy and the gal out. "What about the lawyer?"

"His secretary is dead. We haven't found Anderson."

"Keep looking." He waved the man away and steepled his fingers. This needed to end before Christmas. Romano refused to spend the holiday away from his woman. He grabbed his phone and barked,

"Bring Rosita to me. I want her here." At least if things did go past Christmas, he'd have the comfort at hand's reach.

He jerked his thoughts back to finding a way to get the cowboy and the paralegal off the ranch where he could grab hold of them. He'd have them killed outright if not for the fact he needed to know exactly what they had on him.

Drumming his fingers on the table, he stared out the window at the dreary winter day. Maybe he should relocate to somewhere warm. Florida, maybe. Or California. Plenty of opportunities for a man with his brain for business.

He grinned as an idea came to him, and he again picked up his phone. "Bring me anyone from the ranch. Whoever you see in town first. Take them to the warehouse and send a message to the cowboy that if he doesn't come, the person will be killed." That ought to draw out the rats. Dangling a warning always made a person do what they were supposed to.

~

Mack stared at the two cups of watery brown stuff in front of her. "Hot chocolate made by the twins," Mrs. White had said with a grin. It was up to Mack to choose the winner. Whichever one she chose would get to place the star on the top of the Christmas tree.

"Can't I declare it a tie?"

"No." Mrs. White crossed her arms. "The boys do this every year. They're used to winning or losing."

With a sigh, Mack picked up the cup with the Santa face on it and took a sip. Pretty much flavorless. The drink in the reindeer cup had a bit more sweetness. "Rudolph is the winner."

"Yay." Derrick punched his brother in the arm. "You're the loser."

"If I beat you to the tree, I'm putting the star on." Eric took off at a run, his brother on his heels.

Mack shook her head. "They were both terrible."

"They forgot their recipes, and I'm not allowed to help them. Would you like a good cup of hot chocolate?"

"Coffee is my drink of choice." She removed a cup from the cupboard and filled it with coffee, then added a liberal amount of vanilla creamer.

Through the window, she watched as Deacon and Ryder climbed into the ranch truck to run errands in town. Mack had only been confined to the ranch for one day, and already cabin fever had set in.

"The next contest you'll have to judge—" Mrs. White said. "Is gift wrapping. The boys take a lot of pride in wrapping their parents' gifts."

At least it was something to break up the monotony of not heading to the office every day. The sheriff had all the evidence needed to arrest Romano. The problem now was finding the man. Where would a crime boss hide in Misty Hollow? There weren't any fancy apartments. A few really nice homes, but for the most part, the town was modest, from what she'd seen.

After judging gifts wrapped with far too many bows, she declared Eric the winner this time, whose reward was lighting the big candle in the window later. Mack headed for her tiny house to do some more digging on Romano—anything to escape the holiday-infected house. She'd tried to get into the holiday spirit but failed. With the worry for her brother hanging over her, Christmas seemed more of a trial.

No matter how deep she dug on the internet, she couldn't find anything new on Romano. No clue as to where he might be hiding. She pulled up an aerial view of the hollow and the mountain. There were several secluded homes that looked large enough to provide the man with some of the luxuries he was accustomed to.

Had the sheriff searched those places? Of course, he did. The man was ex-FBI and knew the area. What made Mack think she could do the sheriff's job better than he could?

She groaned and closed her laptop. With her wounded arm out of commission, she couldn't even help with the meals. She was bored. There was no other word for it.

Draping her coat over her shoulders, she went in search of Levi, finding him in the garage with River. Both men peered under hoods of vehicles, greasy rags hanging from back pockets of their jeans.

She'd hoped to find Levi alone, but as she'd backed from the garage, she knocked over a broom.

Both men turned. Levi smiled. "Hey, you. What's up?"

"Nothing." She shrugged. "I'm bored."

"Have a seat. You won't bother us." He turned back to his work.

"That's okay. I'll find something to read." She turned to leave and froze at the sight of a bruised and beaten Ryder shuffling toward them. "Levi."

~

Levi whipped around at the frightened tone in Mack's voice and banged his head on the truck's hood. He put a hand to the already tender spot and followed her gaze. "River, it's Ryder."

111

The three rushed to help him into the warmth of the barn. River dragged over a chair and helped Levi lower their friend onto it.

"What happened?" Levi ran his gaze over the bruises and split lip, the rip in his denim jacket, and the way he held his ribcage.

"Deacon and I were ambushed coming out of the mercantile. Romano's men are holding Deacon in the vacant warehouse off the highway."

"We know the place." It hadn't been long since he and Mack had run from the place in fear of their lives. "I'm guessing you have a message for us."

"Yep. He wants you and Mack. Only the two of you. Then, he'll let Deacon go. If you aren't there by sundown, he'll be killed."

"I'll get the others and Mrs. White to tend to Ryder." River started to leave.

"No. They have to go alone." Ryder struggled to his feet.

"He's right," Levi said. "We can't risk Deacon's life. This isn't his fight." He met Mack's shocked look.

She took a deep shuddering breath and nodded. "I'll get my pepper spray and Taser." She rushed out of the garage.

Useful tools, but Levi wished she carried a gun. Leaving River to tend to their injured friend, Levi sprinted to the bunkhouse to grab his weapon. Within ten minutes, disregarding Dylan's orders to stay, he and Mack sped toward the warehouse.

They had to reach Deacon before the sheriff's department showed up. If the authorities beat them there, his friend's life would be over.

"Well, this could be it," Mack said softly. "Our

chances of making it out alive are very slim."

He took her hand in his. "We'll get out." He wanted to make her a promise but realized how foolish one would be.

The warehouse was eerily silent in the middle of the day and looked even more decrepit without the cover of darkness to hide the chipped block walls and weeds growing through the cracks in the asphalt.

"Which building do you think they're holding Deacon in?"

"I have no idea. I'm hoping they'll come to us." He exited the truck. "Stick close."

"Like glue." She clutched the pepper spray in her good hand.

Since they had no idea which direction to take, Levi led Mack down the center of the compound. No one yelled out or confronted them. They'd used Deacon to lure them here. What kind of game was Romano playing?

The building to their left exploded into flames, then the one on their right. Left, right, each building caught fire. At the end stood three men, one of them a swaying Deacon. Levi pulled his weapon.

"Do you have a plan?" Mack asked.

"Nope. Just grab Deacon and get out."

"What are the fires for?"

"Scare tactics to throw us off our guard."

"Drop the gun." One of the thugs aimed his weapon at Deacon's head.

Levi slowly bent and placed the weapon on the ground.

"Tell me you have another gun," Mack whispered.

"I do." Tucked securely in his waistband.

"Get out of here!" Deacon yelled. "Don't do this for me."

Rather than reply, Levi and Mack continued toward Romano's men, stopping just out of arm's reach. "We're here. Let him go." Levi locked narrowed eyes with the man holding the gun to his friend's head.

The man gave Deacon a shove. Deacon stumbled, almost falling to his knees.

"Keys are in the truck, buddy." Levi jerked his head toward the parking lot.

"Don't do this." Deacon's words fell on deaf ears.

"The two of you come with us." The gun-wielding man motioned them forward.

Mack stepped forward, hand outstretched, and let loose with the pepper spray. The man howled and stumbled back, dropping his weapon. She turned another stream of the spray on the other man.

Levi leaped into action, taking their weapons. "Run." He propped a shoulder under one of Deacon's arms and set off after Mack as fast as he was able.

Curses filled the air behind them, rising above the crackle of flames.

Sirens wailed in the distance.

When Levi glanced back, the two men were nowhere to be seen. They'd managed to get away. This wasn't over, and Romano would try again. The crook now knew that Levi and Mack would come to the rescue of their friends.

They reached his truck as the first of the sheriff's department squad cars roared onto the lot. Sheriff Westbrook and Deputy Hudson exited and marched toward them.

"Glad to see you got him." He narrowed his eyes.

"Don't ever go it alone again."

"Can't promise that." Levi helped Deacon into the truck. "The two men who had him are still in there somewhere unless there's a back way out."

"There is. We'll search, but I'm sure they're gone by now." He motioned for the second squad car to pull up. "Escort these three back to the ranch. Call for backup if you run into trouble."

"Yes, sir." Deputy Young pulled behind Levi's truck.

They needed the escort, but Levi was glad to have it. He grinned through the open truck door at Mack. "Who needs a gun when you're a deadeye with pepper spray?"

She laughed. "I wasn't sure it would work but knew I had to try something."

"I'm glad you did." He climbed into the driver's seat.

"Ryder?" Deacon asked.

"Safe on the ranch." He turned the truck toward Misty Mountain.

"They beat us pretty good before sending him with the message. You shouldn't have come. This could have all turned out a lot differently."

"But it didn't." They might not be as lucky next time. Every encounter with Romano's men would only anger the crime boss more.

"I need more pepper spray," Mack said.

"We'll take Deacon to the clinic, then stop by the mercantile."

"I don't need the clinic." Deacon scowled. "I'm just bruised a bit."

Levi nodded out the window when they reached

the clinic. "Looks like Ryder was brought in. Why else would one of the ranch vehicles be here?"

"Fine. I'll catch a ride home with them."

Mack slid from the truck so Deacon could get out. Once he was inside the clinic, she climbed back in. "What now? What about the next time?"

"We keep doing what we need to until Romano is caught." And pray they didn't die in the process.

Chapter Fifteen

Mack carried breakfast to the two injured men, not surprised to see Levi already there and asking questions. She set the tray on a table and took a seat.

"No mention of where Romano is hiding?" Levi asked.

"Nope." Ryder dug into his stack of pancakes. "Although one of his men did tell the other one that the boss was getting antsy and wanted to put all this behind him. In order to do that, the two of you needed to be dealt with."

"Yep." Deacon refilled his coffee. "Romano doesn't want you killed. He wants to know what you know before killing you."

Mack swallowed against a cotton-filled throat. At least they wouldn't be killed outright. If captured, they might be able to find a way to escape.

"Anyone know much about the local news reporter, Linda Williams?" Levi glanced from one to the other.

"She's always thirsty for a story." Ryder waved his fork, syrup dripping. "Haven't heard anything bad about her, though. No rumors that she's on the take. Why?"

Max, features set in determined lines, locked eyes with Mack. "It's time to stir things up."

"How?" She folded trembling hands in her lap.

"By getting the media involved. Turning up the heat on Romano."

"You want to lure him out." Her skin grew clammy. A dangerous plan but one that might work.

"Yes. I don't want to deal with this on Christmas. We're running out of time." Levi pushed to his feet. "I'm going to send an anonymous email to this reporter and let her take it from there."

Mack trotted after him as he left the bunkhouse. "How much information from the notes are you going to give her?"

"Enough to boil Romano's blood."

They headed to her house where Levi booted up her laptop and went to the *Misty Hollow Gazette*'s website. There he found the reporter's email. Letting her know he wished to remain anonymous to prevent retaliation, he sent her files about Romano lining the pockets of local businessmen and a few on the man's offshore accounts.

"That ought to do it." He sent the email. "She'll do some digging of her own if she's any good and find more that she can add to this."

"People are going to get hurt." Namely Levi if Romano found out he'd alerted the media. Romano didn't need both of them. He might order a hit on Levi and capture Mack rather than both of them. Or...his army could storm the ranch. Either way, everyone Mack had grown to care about would be in danger as soon as Levi hit send.

Later that evening, she and Levi plopped in front

of the television to see whether there was any news about Romano. Dylan and his wife watched with them, having sent the twins to their room to play.

Levi glanced up. "Who told you?"

"Deacon. Are you nuts bringing the media into this?" Dylan scowled.

"This has to end." Levi turned his attention back to the television as the news came on.

Linda Williams stood in front of the sheriff's office. "We received an anonymous tip this morning about the crime boss, Vincent Romano, possibly hiding out in Misty Hollow. The tip included information on his many crimes and offshore accounts." A photo of the man appeared in the top right corner of the screen. "He's ruthless with his hand in drugs, trafficking, and prostitution. He is also allegedly responsible for the disappearance of Alex Anderson of Little Rock."

Mack gasped. How did she find that out?

"What I'd like to know—" Linda continued, "is why our sheriff's department failed to alert the citizens of Misty Hollow that this man was in our midst? He is considered very dangerous. If seen, please contact either the *Misty Hollow Gazette* or Sheriff Westbrook." She stared intently at the camera. "The sister of the victim, Alex Anderson, is residing at the present at the Rocking W Ranch. Perhaps she can come forward and give us more details on this very dangerous man."

Levi turned off the television. "We should prepare ourselves for the media descending on the ranch."

"They won't get past the gate." Dylan marched from the room, Dani at his side.

"He's mad." Mack hung her head. "We should've consulted him before sending that email."

"It's not the boss I'm worried about. That reporter basically announced to the entire town that our sheriff is inept."

~

Romano aimed a gun at the TV and blasted the screen. "Get in here!" He didn't care who. Someone was going to pay.

Two of his men rushed into the room.

"Find Alex. Bring me Sarah. Kill the cowboy. Bring me Mackenzie Anderson. Now!"

They darted from the room.

Romano poured himself a shot of whiskey, downed it, then poured another. Things were spiraling downhill too fast. He'd worked too hard to build his empire to have some two-bit woman and a cowboy bring it all tumbling down.

He needed to get rid of some people. Put a hit on the town's mayor since he'd been approached and promptly turned down Romano's offer. All the mayor had to do was whatever Romano told him, and he'd have more money than he knew what to do with.

What was wrong with these people? Didn't they understand money meant power? Killing a few people would show the rest that he meant business. He grinned. The townspeople were going to be upset with their sheriff after that newscast. Maybe ridding the town of him would be best.

He shook his head. He couldn't willy-nilly order people killed. All he wanted was to get the Anderson woman, find out what she knew, then return to his normal life. Murdering people would only increase what would now become a citywide manhunt. Every yahoo with a gun would be after him.

Strangers stuck out like aliens in small towns. His men had already attracted attention when they went to town for supplies. It was time to move.

He picked up his phone. "Find a remote place in Langley. We're out of here."

~

The late-night news showed riots in town. It looked as if every deputy was on duty and standing in front of the sheriff's office in riot gear.

The scene changed to one of Linda Williams in front of the ranch gate. "We're here to speak with Miss Anderson and have been denied access. You've seen the rioting in our town. The only thing that will stop the rioting is to bring in Romano. To do that, we need to speak to Miss Anderson."

Levi rubbed his hands over the rough whiskers on his face. The reporter gave Mack too much credit. The only way to get to Romano was to use Mack as bait—something he felt sure the reporter wouldn't balk at doing.

"This is getting out of control." Mack leaned her elbows on her knees and stared at the circus on TV. "This isn't going to bring Romano out of hiding. It's going to send him to hide somewhere else."

"Maybe. We've definitely stirred things up."

"Should I meet the reporter at the gate?"

He thought for a minute. "Yes. Let's show Romano that we aren't afraid."

"What do you want me to say?"

"Whatever comes to mind. Talk especially about Alex." He stood and helped her into her coat. "I'm going to wake a couple of the guys to go with us. Everyone needs to know how protected you are. That it won't be easy for Romano to get to you."

"Which means he'll have to get close." She gave him a shaky smile.

"That's the plan." Levi fetched Ryder and Deacon from their beds. It might help their cause to know Romano was responsible for the bruises on the men's faces. They needed all the support of the town they could get, and Levi wasn't above trying to garner sympathy.

Flanked by Deacon and Rydern, all three carrying guns, Levi escorted Mack to the gate. Cameras flashed and Linda Williams turned with a grin.

"Miss Anderson. May we ask you a few questions?"

"No, but I do have something to say." Mack stood ramrod straight. "This is directed to Vincent Romano, the man responsible for the attack on my brother, Alex Anderson, in Little Rock just a couple of weeks ago. Not only that, he's responsible for beating up two of the men you see behind us." Her chin lifted.

"Romano is running scared and taking the cowardly way out, trying to keep me quiet about his crimes. We don't have proof, but we are pretty confident that he is also behind the murder of Rebecca Miller, a lawyer from Little Rock. Now, he's after me and Levi Owens." Mack narrowed her eyes. "Listen to this, Mr. Romano…I will not stop until I find out where my brother is and see that justice is done. Thank you."

She turned and marched back toward the house. Levi had never been prouder.

The reporter shouted questions behind them, but Mack didn't respond. Not until they heard the blare of a siren.

Sheriff Westbrook exited his car and strode through the crowd of photographers. He punched in the code to the gate and strolled through as if he lived there, ignoring Linda's shouts for a statement.

It didn't take a rocket scientist to tell from the look on the sheriff's face that the man was furious. He stormed past them. "In the house." He glanced at Ryder and Deacon as they tried to head for the bunkhouse. "You, too."

Like kids being called to the principal's office, the four of them followed. Dylan waited in the living room.

The sheriff crossed his arms and glared. "If you don't think I'm doing a good enough job, you could've come to me instead of turning the town against me."

"That wasn't our intention." Levi lowered to the couch.

"Nor did you tell me about Ryder and Deacon's beating. The more evidence we have against Romano, the better. Then, the fiasco tonight outside the gate." He turned his attention to Mack. "Do you have a death wish?"

"No, the opposite." She hitched her chin. "Romano isn't going to show himself without provocation. We're helping you."

"Hindering is more like it. I ought to arrest both of you."

"We've turned over all the evidence." Levi shot to his feet. "We aren't withholding information. Christmas is coming, Sheriff. We'd like to enjoy the holiday without the threat of Romano."

"Stupid reasoning." He shook his head. "I've got a lot of damage control to do. It would've been nice if you'd have put in a good word during your little press conference." His shoulders slumped. "Thought the two of you should know that we think Romano has left Misty Hollow. Several unknown vehicles were spotted leaving. If not for the riots in town, I could've sent some deputies to follow them. Now, we start all over in our search. Goodnight." He left, slamming the door behind him on his way out.

"I feel bad now." Mack sighed.

"Maybe we did jump the gun a bit." Levi slumped against the back of the sofa. Hearing that Romano had left town wasn't good. Their plan on luring him into a trap hadn't worked. Instead, he was hiding under another rock.

"What now?" Levi asked.

"I don't know. We wait and see, I guess. Maybe once Romano settles somewhere, we'll hear from him." At least it would be safe to go into town again.

His resolve to tie up things before Christmas might not happen. He'd really wanted to make Christmas even more special by helping Mack get justice for Alex.

He'd failed.

Chapter Sixteen

A knock sounded on her door. Mack glanced at the clock. She still had half an hour before she needed to be in the kitchen with Mrs. White.

Frowning, she peered through the peephole, then she blinked. What she saw didn't register. Alex?

She yanked open the door. "Alex!" She threw her arms around him, then noted Willy standing off to the side.

"This all right?" He asked.

"More than all right, Willy. Thank you." She pulled her brother into the house. "You have some explaining to do."

He lowered himself gingerly to the sofa, one arm wrapped around his midsection. "I'd rather tell everything once if you don't mind getting Levi."

She thundered up the stairs to where she'd left her phone and sent a quick text before changing out of the flannel pajamas she'd slept in. Dressed in fleece-lined leggings and a baggy sweater, she rejoined her brother.

"I'm so glad to see you." She sat next to him. "I knew you weren't dead. I felt it in my heart."

He put an arm around her shoulder. "I came close

a few times."

The door burst open. Levi, a shocked look on his face, stood there and stared. "Dude."

"Bro." Alex grinned. "Thanks for taking care of my little sister."

"Anytime." Levi closed the door and pulled up a chair across from them. "Rebecca Miller is dead."

Alex's face fell. "That hurts." He leaned his head against the back of the sofa. "Can I have a cup of coffee? Maybe something to eat?"

Mack jumped up and poured him a cup of coffee before toasting two pieces of bread. "This ought to hold you over until breakfast. Now talk."

"You were there when I was attacked."

"Yes, and I saw you stabbed more than once." Guilt again ripped through her at the memory that she'd run.

"Those two thugs left me for dead and ran when they heard sirens. Knowing that going to the hospital would be a death sentence, I forced myself to get up and run." He closed his eyes. "Didn't think I'd make it to my apartment much less the lake house."

"We found evidence you were there," Levi said.

Alex grinned. "I knew you'd think about that place. Anyway, I holed up there until I regained some strength, then hopped from cheap motel to cheap motel until I saw the press conference last night." He turned his attention to Mack. "It's not a good idea to taunt Romano, Sis."

"This has gone on long enough. Was me talking to the press what brought you out of hiding?"

"Yep, I came to stop the two of you from doing something stupid. I'm assuming you found the files on the man?"

"We did."

"Then you've handed them to the authorities. Let them take things from here."

Mack scowled. "They aren't doing enough fast enough. Sheriff Westbrook is good, but Romano stays one step ahead. If we can lure him into the open, then the police can arrest him, and we can go back to our normal lives." Mack turned away at her words. What had she said?

"I'm begging you, Mackenzie. Let this go."

"Stay in hiding for the rest of my life?" She planted her fists on her hips. "No."

He struggled to his feet. "I need to get going. My presence here is too dangerous."

"No more so than me being here. Talk some sense into him, Levi."

Levi faced them. "She's right. There's no safer place than the Rocking W. Everyone here is armed, and there are security cameras everywhere...you're safe here."

"It would be nice to have a place to heal." Alex thrust his hand toward his friend.

"None of that." Levi wrapped him in a hug. "We're family. Come on. There's an extra bed in the bunkhouse. You can clean up before breakfast. Believe it or not, Mack helps out in the kitchen."

Alex spewed out a laugh. "That's not something I thought I'd ever hear."

"Ha ha." Mack followed them out the door, then watched as Levi slowed his long pace to match her brother's shuffling one. Confident her brother was in good hands, she hurried to help Mrs. White and

Marilyn in the kitchen and let them know to set a plate for one more.

~

Levi replaced a tire on one of the tractors while River worked on another. He couldn't believe Alex was alive. His friend definitely looked like he'd been dragged behind a horse and stomped on a few times. He could heal here, though, and Mack could stop worrying about him. His arrival would make her Christmas a little merrier.

"You about finished?" River wiped his hands on a rag. "It's our turn to ride the perimeter of the ranch."

"Yep." Then he would check on Alex. His friend had been sound asleep since breakfast.

After saddling their horses, the two rode side by side around the ranch, noting places where the fence needed mending and keeping an eye out for sick or wounded livestock.

"Mack's brother's been through some stuff," River said.

"Yep."

"I never thought being a lawyer could be such a dangerous job. Makes me glad to be a mechanic on a ranch."

Levi chuckled. "We've had our share of danger."
"Every time a pretty gal comes to town." River laughed. "Sure seems that way, doesn't it? Are you going to marry Mack?"

Levi jerked. "Why do you ask that?"

"The others married the women they protected." River shrugged. "Figured you'd fall into the same trap."

"Haven't thought about it." Liar. "Mack has always been like a little sister to me." Another lie.

Once, maybe, but when he'd visited Alex on a college break, he'd noted what a beautiful woman Mack was becoming. Then, she'd shown up here, pain written across her face, and he'd known she was far more than a little sister. "Besides, she'll be heading back to Little Rock once the danger is over."

"Maybe not. Anything can happen."

Levi's horse snorted and tossed his head, dancing sideways. "Whoa, boy."

"Something has them spooked." River pulled on the reins, then slid from the saddle. "Might be a dead animal."

"Most likely." Levi followed suit, securing the reins to the fence.

He sniffed, not detecting the ripe odor of death. What had spooked the horses? It was too cold for snakes. "A coyote maybe?"

"Not unless coyotes wear flowered sweaters." River pointed under a juniper bush. "We've got a body here."

Levi climbed through the barbed wire fence and peered into the brush. Sharon's sightless eyes stared back at him.

"Do you know her?" River asked.

"Yep. She's the receptionist who turned against Alex and Mack." Romano must not have needed her anymore. "Call the sheriff."

Most of the ranch had joined them before the sheriff arrived. Mack stood close to her brother who looked stricken. "She was a plant from Romano?" Alex shook his head. "She's worked for me since day one."

"Maybe he made her an offer she couldn't refuse." Mack peered into her brother's face. "She might not have always worked for him."

"This is a warning, Sis. If you don't let things go, you could end up like her."

Levi wanted to agree, but they'd gone too far. Quitting now would not stop a man like Romano.

Willy arrived in the side-by-side with Sheriff Westbrook. Levi gave him the woman's identity, then stepped back to let the sheriff take over.

"Looks like she was shot execution style." The sheriff turned as two men in EMT jackets arrived in another side-by-side.

They zipped Sharon into a body bag and attached her to a board on the back of the all-terrain vehicle. "We'll let you know what the autopsy shows," one of them said, "but it is obvious as to the cause of death."

The sheriff turned to Levi. "What's your plan now? Don't tell me you don't have one. Plus, I want to see footage of any camera that might show this area."

Levi glanced at one mounted to a nearby tree. "Whoever dumped her didn't care about the cameras."

"No, but more evidence against Romano and his men is a good thing. We have enough to put him away for a long time. All we need to do now is find him."

"Should we set a trap?" A stubborn look crossed Mack's face.

"No, we should not." Alex scowled.

"Who are you?" The sheriff narrowed his eyes.

Levi made the introductions. "As much as it turns my blood to ice water, Mack is right. A trap is the only way to get to Romano. We can wear wires. Set up video surveillance ahead of the meeting. Your department will see and hear us the entire time."

Sheriff Westbrook rubbed his chin. "Fine, but we

choose the place. The warehouse Romano liked using is nothing but a burned-out pile of rubble now. Let me get back to you this afternoon. Come to the office and we'll finalize the details."

Three hours later, Levi, Mack, and Alex entered the conference room of the sheriff department. Westbrook raised an eyebrow at Alex's presence, but he didn't ask him to leave.

Good. Romano wanted Alex as much or more than he did Levi and Mack.

"Law enforcement in Langley and Little Rock have agreed to help us. There is a vacant office building in Langley we can use. As we speak, cameras are being set in place." He unrolled a blueprint. "Study the layout of this building. If things go south, you need to know your way out. I doubt Romano will show alone, but be prepared." He glanced at Alex. "I assume you're going?"

"Yes, sir. I'm the tastiest bait." He breathed deeply through his nose. "I'm doing this reluctantly, though."

"At least one of the three of you has a bit of common sense."

"What time do you want us to set the meeting for?" Mack asked.

"Romano likes the cover of darkness, so let's say ten p.m. tomorrow. I want everyone in place by nine. If you have a gun, bring it. Romano won't expect you to show up empty-handed."

"I'll pack my new can of pepper spray." Mack gave a nod.

The sheriff grinned. "Which I heard came in handy the other day. The three of you stick together like superglue. Do not allow yourselves to be separated. Your safety depends on us knowing where you are at all times." He glanced at Alex again. "You up to this? Heard about your attack."

"I'm good. No vital organs were hit, and I'm getting stronger every day."

Sheriff Westbrook didn't look convinced. "You could jeopardize the whole thing if you collapse."

"I won't."

"We won't leave him behind." Mack crossed his arms.

"That's why he's a hindrance. Here's the address to the meeting place. Before going there, meet us in front of the supermarket to wire up. Then, you'll head to the warehouse where law enforcement will already be planted." He placed his palms flat on the table. "This is it. If we fail, we might not get another chance. Let's put Romano behind bars."

Mack couldn't agree more. Despite the danger, he couldn't help but feel an element of excitement. Tomorrow could very well end the nightmare of Romano's empire. He put a hand on the small of Mack's back and guided her to his truck.

Alex glanced from Levi's hand to his face, then arched a brow. "Anything I need to know?"

"Nope." Now was not the time to tell his friend how he felt about Mack. Not until he knew whether he could persuade her to stay in Misty Hollow. The town he loved would not be the same without her. All they had to do was make it through tomorrow, and he'd tell her.

Maybe on Christmas.

Chapter Seventeen

Mack, Levi, and Alex spent the time before meeting Romano by wiring up and making sure they knew where all the exits were in case they needed to run. She glanced in corners as she passed cameras that looked like anything but. Wasp nests, shattered mirrors...Despite the precautions set in place to keep her and Levi safe, perspiration trickled down her spine under the Kevlar vest she wore.

"It'll be okay." Levi put an arm around her waist and gave her a quick squeeze.

"Don't lie." Alex glared. "We could all die tonight. Romano won't like being lured into a trap. He'll retaliate."

"Not if he's behind bars," Levi said. "We have to make sure he's arrested."

Mack agreed with Levi. If they failed in catching Romano, the fallout would be severe. They couldn't let him escape.

"Everything is ready." Sheriff Westbrook joined them. "Remember...do not allow yourselves to be separated. We want Romano with you when we storm the place."

"Do you want us to get him to confess to the murders of Rebecca Miller and Sarah?" Mack asked.

"If you can. We have enough evidence from the files you gave me to convict him, but the more nails in his coffin, the better." The sheriff sighed. "Be careful. Keep your wits about you. I have to stay out of sight. He should show in fifteen minutes."

"But, there's half an hour until—"

"He'll show early." Alex drew a sharp breath through his nose. "In case of a trap."

"Oh." Mack should've known. Romano was too savvy not to expect a trap. "What do we do until he shows?" she asked after the sheriff left.

"Worry about what's going to happen." Her brother leaned against a wall. "Let's hope he doesn't shoot at the sight of me."

"Maybe you should stand behind me." Levi grinned.

"It's not funny. Romano doesn't take well to betrayal."

Mack's heart rate increased as the minutes ticked away. When the meeting time came and went, her legs trembled. Romano wasn't coming. "Where is he?"

"He'll be here." Despite the threat of danger, Levi seemed relaxed. He leaned against a wall, arms and legs crossed. If not for the way his eyes darted around the room, she'd think him oblivious to what could happen.

Another half an hour passed before the sound of a slamming car door reached her ears. Alex and Levi pushed away from the wall. The three of them faced the door as Romano and two armed thugs entered the building.

"Those are the men that attacked me," Alex

whispered.

The man's gaze landed on Alex and hardened. "So, it's true. You're alive."

Alex shrugged. "Sorry to disappoint you."

"Where is the evidence against me?"

"Locked up for safekeeping." Mack released a shuddering breath, doing her best not to show fear.

Romano crossed his arms. "Then why am I here?"

"I didn't say it wasn't here. I said it was safe."

"Give it to me so we can be done with this."

Mack glanced at Levi, then back to Romano. "What do we get in exchange?"

The man's eyes narrowed. "Isn't your life enough? Or maybe you aren't as morally motivated as your brother."

"I've seen what crossing you does." She gave a thin-lipped smile. "I also think you owe us compensation for giving you the files and ordering an attack on my brother. Not to mention you had Rebecca and Sarah killed."

"They betrayed me." He shrugged.

"So, you admit to killing them?"

"I didn't kill them per se."

"No, you had someone else do your dirty work." Come on and confess.

He sighed. "Why do you care, Miss Anderson? They were expendable."

Was that enough of a confession? She hoped so.

"Enough jabbering." Levi turned. "Follow me."

"Wait." Alex stopped them. "Romano isn't a liar. Before we turn over what he wants, we need his word that he'll let us leave here safely."

Mack arched a brow. "An honest crook?"

Romano laughed. "When a person has the power I do, there's no reason to lie. Yes, I give my word the three of you can go once I have what I came for. But, if you so much as stick one toe in my business again, I'll have you cut into pieces and fed to the fish."

"Our compensation?" Mack crossed her arms.

His laughter increased. "You are persistent, Miss Anderson. You should come work for me."

"No thanks."

"Fine. One hundred thousand."

"Each."

His eyes widened, but his grin didn't fade. "Very well." He jerked his head toward one of the men who then left the building.

"You keep that kind of cash on you?" Mack frowned.

"A man never knows when he has a deal to make."

Once the man returned with a duffel bag, Levi led them down a hallway to where the trap for Romano would go down. They entered a larger warehouse storeroom with a tall metal filing cabinet against one wall. Copies of the evidence given to the sheriff awaited in one of the drawers. As soon as Levi handed it over, the waiting law enforcement would storm inside.

Levi had chosen the room because of the crates piled around that would give them cover should Romano and his men start shooting. He headed toward the cabinet as Mack reached for the duffel bag. A glance over his shoulder showed Alex hanging back, clearly uncomfortable.

"Not until I see the files." Romano shook his head

toward the man with the money.

Levi pulled a key from his pocket and unlocked the top drawer, then he lifted out the files. "It's all here."

~

The thug threw the duffel bag at Mack's feet.

Romano took the files. "Much obliged. We're done here."

"Halt! Police." A side door burst open, and a handful of law enforcement officers burst inside. Another group came through the same door Levi and the others had.

Levi grabbed Mack's hand. "Let's get out of here."

"The money." She lifted the duffel bag. "It's too light."

Romano dove behind the filing cabinet as his men opened fire.

The police officers did the same.

Levi dragged Mack behind a pile of crates and pulled his weapon. Alex dove after them. "Stay down. Stay here with Alex."

She pulled her pepper spray from her pocket. "Be careful."

"I don't plan on joining the fight, Sweetheart. I'm making sure you don't get hurt or that Romano escapes." Keeping low, he left them and, staying close to the walls, headed to where he'd seen the man take cover.

He jumped behind the cabinet. Romano was gone. Where? Levi scanned the area.

Bullets pinged the other side of the cabinet. He ducked. Then, keeping his back plastered against the cabinet, he peered around it to a side door closing.

He darted across the room and yanked the door open. "I'm going after Romano." Hopefully, the sheriff could get free to provide him with backup. Good thing was, Levi had been through the building before. Romano hadn't.

He stopped and listened, expecting a bullet to slam into him. When one didn't come, he went right. The scuff of a shoe in the other direction had him changing to go that way. With Romano's men busy fighting with law enforcement, the only person who could be out other than Levi was the man he sought.

If Romano got away, he'd come after Mack and Alex with a vengeance. Levi, too. No one on the ranch would be safe.

Levi peered in each room he passed. Most were empty of anywhere to hide. When he reached a room that offered a few hiding places such as a desk and closet, he slowly entered, his weapon held at the ready.

"You can't get away, Romano. Come on out."

A bullet slammed into his chest, taking his breath away. Man, that hurt. He fell to his knees, then dropped, swiveling to train his own gun on Romano's face. Sneaky, coming up behind him. Luckily it had hit his Kevlar.

Romano stared him down. "Bullet-proof vest? I should've known you'd set a trap for me." He aimed for Levi's head.

Levi shot twice, striking the man in his gun arm, then again in his leg. Having disarmed him, he kicked the other man's gun out of reach. "We had to. We couldn't let you get away."

The gunfire from the other room had stopped,

signaling the end of the gunfight.

Levi suppressed the urge to wince against the pain. "I'm pretty sure your men are dead. They were severely outnumbered."

"I've got more men." Roman held a hand to his wounded arm and lifted his chin. "You'll pay for this."

"I doubt it. You might be able to do a little from behind bars, but your empire will be disbanded. Your men arrested. Your sordid businesses shut down." He reached into the man's jacket and pulled out the file. "Make yourself comfortable. The sheriff will be here soon." Levi perched on the corner of the desk, keeping his gun trained on Romano.

"I should've had you killed."

"Seems to me you tried a couple of times." Levi glanced up as the sheriff and Deputy Hudson entered the room. "Good. I'm heading back to Mack. Romano is all yours."

"Good work, Levi." The sheriff pulled a pair of cuffs from his belt and cuffed the other man despite his protests that he'd been shot. "Shut up before I shoot you again."

Chuckling, Levi rushed to find Mack. The battle room now held dead Romano thugs and a few law enforcement officers standing over them.

He found Alex and Mack outside. He held his arms wide, and Mack rushed into them.

"Thank God. I heard shots and feared the worst."

"Kevlar protected me. Romano not so much." He waved to a waiting paramedic. "The man can't walk on his own."

With a nod, the medic called to another. They rolled a gurney into the building.

"It's over." Her words sounded muffled against his chest.

"Well, there'll be a trial. That probably won't take place until after Christmas. Guess you'll have to stick around another week or two."

She smiled up at him. "I don't mind at all."

"Is there something the two of you need to tell me?" Alex frowned.

"No," They said in unison.

Soon, Levi would tell Mack what she meant to him and ask her to stay, but not yet. There were still loose ends to tie up.

"Hmm." Alex didn't look convinced. "Seems I have some thinking to do."

"Like what?" Mack glanced at him.

"You aren't the only ones with secrets." He smirked and headed for the truck.

Levi started to ask what he meant but closed his mouth as the medics wheeled a cursing Romano from the building. As he passed, he shouted out a diatribe of revenge.

Mack scowled and threw the duffel bag at him. "Don't want your blood money. I was just going to give it to charity."

Romano told her what she could do with her charity, then resumed his cursing as he was lifted into the ambulance. Once he was inside, the medics returned to the building with body bags.

"Good job." Sheriff Westbrook removed his cowboy hat and wiped his brow. "Dirty gunfight, but I didn't lose any deputies. One officer from Langley suffered a flesh wound, but all in all, they did a great job. Have a great Christmas."

"You, too," Mack and Levi said in unison.

With Alex nowhere in sight, Levi lowered his head and planted a heated kiss on Mack. Breathless, he straightened. "Let's go home and celebrate getting Romano off the streets before Christmas."

"That sounds wonderful." She gave him another quick kiss, then headed for the truck.

Chapter Eighteen

Christmas morning dawned crisp and bright. Snow had fallen during the night turning the ranch into a winter wonderland.

Mack let the curtains fall into place and padded downstairs to wake her brother for their customary Christmas morning coffee. "Wakey-wakey. Merry Christmas."

Alex groaned and pulled the blankets over his head.

Laughing, Mack started making the coffee. The aroma would wake her brother soon enough. "I don't have a gift for you," she said when the coffee was done. She handed him a cup.

"That's okay, Sis. I don't have anything for you either." He sat up and tossed the blankets off the couch. "This is not the most comfortable thing to sleep on, by the way."

"Sorry." She dropped into the chair across from him. "Having you back is the best gift, Alex. I was so worried."

"I might have something in the works you'll like." He blew on his drink. "Can't say too much right now."

"I'm intrigued." She dropped her gaze to her cup. Please, no more secrets.

"Don't worry, little Sis." He grinned. "If it works out, I guarantee you'll like what I'm doing."

"Hmmm."

"So, what's up for the day?"

"After breakfast, everyone gathers in the main house to exchange gifts." She'd placed her wrapped gifts under the tree the day before.

"I'll stay here. No need for a person who has nothing to give."

"You will not. Breakfast is homemade cinnamon rolls, and today is not the day to be alone." She stood and set her cup in the sink. "I'm going to shower and get ready, then you can while I help Mrs. White."

"Great." He placed his cup on the coffee table and lay back on the sofa.

"Don't fall back asleep. I'm serious about you joining the festivities."

"Yeah, yeah."

After her shower, Mack donned a red sweater and black jeans. After she made sure her brother headed for the shower, she rushed out into the cold to help with breakfast.

"Merry Christmas," she chirped upon entering the kitchen.

Mrs. White and Marilyn smiled and repeated the greeting.

"What a change arresting Romano has had on you." Mrs. White handed her an apron.

"It's a great weight off my shoulders. That and having my brother back alive." She tied the apron on and gathered the ingredients for frosting the buns.

"After breakfast," Mrs. White said, "the day is all yours. You can attend the gift exchange or not. It isn't mandatory, although everyone does go. There's hot chocolate." She smiled.

"Yours or the twins'?" Mack arched a brow.

"Mine."

"Good. Then, I'll be there."

"What's so funny?" Levi came through the back door, stomping snow from his boots.

"Hot chocolate." Mack's smile widened.

"Really? Merry Christmas." He planted a soft kiss on her cheek and pulled a small, wrapped box from under his coat. "For you. Later."

"Looks like jewelry." Marilyn waggled her eyebrows.

"Why would Levi buy me jewelry?" Her face heated. Was it? Dare she hope he wanted her to stay?

The decision to return to Little Rock or remain in Misty Hollow had plagued her in the few days since Romano's arrest. To stay, she needed to know that Levi wanted her to.

What would she do here? She couldn't stay on the ranch. Maybe she could rent a house in town, offer paralegal advice, and work online. Mack shrugged and put away the powdered sugar and milk. She didn't have to decide today. Romano's trial wasn't until after New Year's.

Alex arrived right as everyone was sitting down to eat. He slid onto a chair next to Mack. "Smells good. What part did you do?"

"The frosting."

"Ah. No cooking. Good." He grinned, glancing at the others around the table. "Cooking is not one of her talents."

Mack punched his shoulder. "Hush."

"A gal can't be good at everything." Levi tossed her a wink.

"She's learning," Marilyn spoke up. "Mack's come a long way in the short time she's been here."

"Whoa." Alex held up his hands. "I surrender. I had no idea my little sister was one of y'all. Thank you for looking after her in my absence."

"A friend of Levi's is a friend of ours," Dylan said. "That makes you one of us. Eat up. Presents await, and the twins are getting restless."

Mack's mind returned to the gift Levi had set under the tree. Hope leaped in her heart. Maybe the present would give her the answer to her dilemma.

After everyone ate, she helped the other two women clean up, then joined the rest in the large living room. Candles set a pleasant ambiance along with the lights on the Christmas tree. The twins sat near the pile of gifts, prepared to play Santa.

"Here." Levi patted the arm of the chair he sat on.

She perched on it, leaning an arm on his shoulder. "I've never celebrated with this many people before."

"I know. It used to be just us three and your parents. Then, just us in college. Intimate celebrations are nice, but so is this." He placed a hand on her bent knee. "The day is more special having you and Alex to celebrate with again." He smiled up at her.

"Thank you for helping me. I wasn't sure what to expect when I arrived at the Rocking W."

"I'll always be here for you, Sweetheart." He lifted her hand to his lips.

"Let's hope we never have to go through anything

like we did with Romano."

"You might, considering your career. With Alex being a prosecutor—"

She nodded. "I wish he'd go back to being a defense attorney. Safer."

"Here." Eric dropped the gift Mack had purchased for Levi onto his lap, then handed her the one from him.

Dylan and his wife, Dani, had given all those who worked on the ranch healthy bonuses for Christmas. "For the first time since we started, the ranch made a very healthy profit," the boss said. "The summer camps, camping trips, and livestock is paying off, thanks to all your hard work. Merry Christmas." He raised a glass of Champagne in a toast.

"Merry Christmas," everyone said at once.

~

Levi opened the gift from Mack. "You remembered what I like to read."

"Of course. When you and Alex weren't out causing trouble, you always had your nose in a book." She untied the ribbon around the box he'd given her.

Inside the box lay an engraved ink pen. "To my Big Mack." Tears welled in her eyes.

"I bought that for you the day you started college, but then I found out you were dating someone and didn't think it would be appropriate. I know you hate that nickname, but can't it be what I call you? In private?"

She nodded. "I didn't date in college. Someone lied to you."

Levi glanced at Alex, who shrugged. "Sorry, dude. I didn't want you dating my little sister."

"That should've been left up to her to decide." He

clenched his jaw tight enough to make his teeth hurt. Did he still feel that way?

"Again, I'm sorry. I was young and stupid."

Levi turned back to Mack who stared at the pen. Did she like it? He couldn't tell if her tears were ones of joy or sadness.

"Excuse me." She rushed from the room, taking the pen with her.

Levi started to follow, but Alex stopped him. "Let me. She's mad at me." He clapped Levi on the shoulder, then rushed after his sister.

Levi sat back down and halfway watched as the twins opened their gifts. They seemed happy to receive the books Mack gave them, but set them aside in favor of BB guns their father gave them.

Once the boys finished opening their gifts, everyone filed from the room, leaving the Wyatt family alone. Levi headed for the barn. A ride around the ranch might clear his head so he could decipher Mack's reaction to his gift.

Was she upset that the engraving said Big Mack? Maybe he'd overstepped the boundaries of friendship by having that engraved on something she'd use every day.

He saddled his horse, then led it from the barn before swinging onto the saddle. As he passed Mack's house, he spotted her and Alex through the window. They seemed to be in a heated conversation.

Maybe his friend was right. Maybe Mack was upset with the lie he'd told her in college.

His breath plumed in front of him in the cold air. The horse's hooves crunched through the crust on top of the snow. Cardinals flitted through the trees, lending more to the Christmas atmosphere. The area looked like a Christmas card.

After an hour and feeling more peaceful, he returned to the barn and soothed his flustered nerves further by brushing his horse's coat. Until Alex entered. Then his blood started to boil again. "Who is she upset with?" He asked.

"Me. After some yelling, she started to ramble." He plopped onto a stool. "She started shouting about how things could've been different, how I might've ruined her life, blah blah blah. None of it made much sense to me other than she said I ruined Christmas." His shoulders slumped. "Told me to move back to the bunkhouse."

Levi wasn't sure he wanted his friend there any more than Mack wanted him in her house. "Would it have been so wrong for me to date your sister?"

"No, but I didn't know that then. I thought it would change our friendship. Has it?"

"I am upset—"

"I'm talking about your feelings for Mackenzie now, not then."

"Who said—"

Alex shook his head. "Stop denying it. I've seen the way the two of you look at each other. How you kiss How protective you are of her. Sending her to you was a good idea." He smiled.

"It's all a moot point. She'll be returning to Little Rock with you. That's where her career is."

"A lot can happen in a couple of weeks." Alex stood. "I'm working on something."

"Nothing that will bring more trouble, I hope." Levi narrowed his eyes.

"No, nothing like that. I'll let you know once things are in place." He grinned and sauntered out of the barn, whistling a Christmas carol.

The sound of the cowbell announcing the Christmas meal pulled him reluctantly from the barn. Mack was right. Exposing Alex's lie had put a pall over Christmas.

The aroma of roast turkey greeted him. Mrs. White knew how to put up a holiday spread. His stomach rumbled despite the lack of excitement over seeing Alex across the dining table. Not to mention he had no idea how Mack was going to act toward either him or her brother.

He sat in his usual chair as the women carried platters of food into the room. His gaze met Mack's as she set a bowl of gravy on the table.

"I'm sorry," she mouthed. "Later?"

He nodded, his spirit brightening. She wasn't upset with him.

After a meal that left him stuffed, Levi stepped onto the back deck to wait for Mack. He leaned on the railing, his gaze sweeping over the ranch as snow began to fall. "You got your white Christmas," he said as Mack joined him.

"It's beautiful." She leaned her back against the railing and faced him. Snowflakes landed in her hair and on her eyelashes. "I'm not upset about the pen, Levi. It's lovely and I appreciate the sentiment, I really do."

"But?" He held his breath.

"Alex's confession threw me." Her gaze locked with his. "What do you think would've happened if he hadn't told you I was dating someone?"

He smiled. "We'd have done a whole lot more of this. Merry Christmas, Mackenzie." He stepped in front of her and cupped her face. Her eyes closed and her lips parted. Levi lowered his head and kissed her. Softly, tenderly, then with a growing passion that made him forget about the snow landing on his shoulders. The heat of the kiss kept him warm enough.

Chapter Nineteen

Mack smoothed the blazer that matched the navy skirt she wore. She frowned. Coming her way was a rival attorney. Although the man was one of the most respected in the state, he reminded her of an ambulance chaser with his smirk and smoothed-back hair.

"Hello, Ronald. I shouldn't be surprised to find you representing Romano. Once upon a time, you prosecuted the dirt bags." She hitched her chin.

"I go where the money is, darlin'." He thrust out his hand. "Where's that brother of yours?"

"Don't worry. He'll be here." She resisted the urge to wipe her hand on her skirt after he withdrew his hand. "He won't want to miss the trial."

"Right. A victim and all that." The man's smirk widened. "I'll find holes in the evidence you submitted."

"No, you won't." It was her turn to smile. "Not a hole in sight, but, I'm sure you know that. You don't care whether Romano walks or not. I'm guessing you took your payment up front."

He laughed. "You're a smart girl, Miss Anderson. See you in the courtroom."

She watched him go and shuddered. Ronald Oglesby would be a formidable enemy. While she didn't keep it a secret as to her dislike of him, she kept it bordering on civility. Better he think her unfriendly than hostile. Especially since he'd be examining her on the witness stand.

Nothing could go wrong today. No hung jury. The verdict had to be unanimous that Romano was guilty on all counts.

"Ready, Sis?" Alex rushed toward her. "Levi will be inside as support." He straightened his tie.

"Are you upset that you're not the prosecutor today?"

"No, I make a better witness under the circumstances." He gave her a quick one-armed hug.

They entered the courtroom and headed to their seats. Amy Laken, a middle-aged woman, well-known in the state, entered next. She'd love a victory against Oglesby.

Levi sat in the first row behind them. His smile calmed the nerves in her stomach.

"You never have told me about your secret," she said to her brother. "The one you mentioned on Christmas."

"I'll tell you after the jury reaches a verdict. Hopefully, in a few days. We need to focus now."

She twisted her hands in her lap, then picked up a pencil and tapped it on the table, until Amy glanced at her and shook her head. With a sigh, she refolded her hands in her lap and tried not to fidget.

The judge, Marcus Johnson, entered the room.

"All stand," the bailiff announced.

Once the judge sat, so did everyone else. Then a

handcuffed Romano was brought into the room and sat next to Oglesby. "The state versus Vincent Romano case number eight sixteen." The bailiff took his place next to the judge. "Charges of murder, trafficking..." the list seemed as long as Mack's arm.

Lakey gave her opening statement, pushing hard on the murders Romano had ordered, then went into his years of organized crime. The faces of the jury settled into hard lines.

Oglesby followed with a short opening statement focusing on how much money Romano put into the state with his donations. Not really having anything else to try and make the criminal more likeable, he turned things over to Amy.

"The defendant may donate money to several charities," she told the jury, "But I will show you today the true nature of Vincent Romano. A man who hires others to do his dirty work. A man who sells men, women, and children as if they were property. A man who fills our streets with drugs. This great city of Little Rock and the state of Arkansas will be better once this horrible man is behind bars. Thank you."

She nodded at Oglesby who shrugged, then resumed her seat.

After the police gave an account of the case, Alex was called to the stand. He raised his right hand and swore to tell the truth, then sat in the witness chair.

~

Oglesby approached him. "Is it true you considered working for Romano? I mean, a man who claims to be upright would've denied his offer outright, wouldn't he? Why did you wait weeks before saying no to working for the defendant?"

153

"I dug into his dealings and decided I wanted no part of it."

"But you did work for him for a short time?"

"Not exactly. "More like a handful of meetings.""

"So, you were an associate of his?"

"I wouldn't call myself that." Alex's gaze landed on Mack.

Her throat seized. If Oglesby made the jury believe that her brother had worked for Romano, they wouldn't believe his testimony.

"What would you call yourself, Mr. Anderson?"

"A man who knows right from wrong and wants to see justice served."

"You mean a man who stretches the truth." Oglesby raised a brow toward the jury. "No further questions."

Amy approached the witness bench. "Isn't it true, Mr. Anderson, that you met with Romano in order to find out what he was up to and how you could acquire the information to put him behind bars?"

"Objection," Oglesby shouted. "She's leading the witness."

"Quiet, Mr. Oglesby. You know that isn't the case here. Be careful, Miss Laken."

"My apologies, Your Honor." She smiled at Alex. "Mr. Anderson, please tell the jury why you met with the defendant."

"Romano wanted me to work for him. After a couple of meetings, I realized how deep he was into the crime in Little Rock. I started digging for information. A man like him does not deserve to walk free."

"What information did you find on the defendant?"

"Drug deals, prostitution, trafficking...murder."

"In fact, Mr. Anderson, there was an attempt at murder on your life. Isn't that correct?"

"Yes. I barely made it out of that alley alive, then went into hiding to protect my sister." He glanced at Mack.

"No more questions, Your Honor." Amy returned to her seat beside Mack.

"The defense calls the next witness, Mackenzie Anderson."

Mack stood.

"Just answer his questions," Amy said. "Oglesby knows there is no way Romano can walk free."

Mack nodded, took a deep breath, and swore to tell the truth. As she sat, her gaze landed on Levi. He smiled and winked.

Nothing could happen to her there. She was safe. Soon, the whole horrible ordeal would be over, and she could decide what her future would look like.

~

Levi shifted in his seat, a knot forming between his shoulder blades. Despite the mounting evidence against Romano, the man seemed relaxed. As if he believed he'd walk out of the courtroom a free man.

Levi glanced around the room behind him. Every seat was filled. Mostly with men, but a few women sat in the back row. Something sinister hovered over the proceedings.

The prosecutor stepped forward, pulling Levi's attention back to the trial.

"Miss Anderson. Please tell the courtroom, in your own words, what happened on the day you ended up on the Rocking W Ranch in Misty Hollow and what you discovered once you arrived there. Tell us everything you can remember."

"I had my customary weekly supper with my brother. He told me if anything happened to him, to go to his friend, Levi Owens, on the ranch. He said Romano had asked him to work for him and after a few meetings, Levi turned him down.

"After we ate, we walked home as usual. In an alley, two men cornered us. Alex told me to run. I glanced over my shoulder to see the two men stabbing him. He fell. Sirens rang out in the distance. I ran. The men chased me a short way, then disappeared." She took a deep shuddering breath. "I collected some things from my apartment and headed for Misty Hollow."

Levi remembered the frightened woman who had arrived on the ranch. Despite her moments of fear, she'd done what needed doing when the time came.

"Levi and I went to the office I shared with my brother and found the files he'd made on Romano. Then, our receptionist set up a meeting with Romano which turned out to be a trap. Levi and I barely made it out with our lives. Rebecca Miller did not." She went on to tell about working with local law enforcement to set a trap for Romano.

"And you gave these files to Sheriff Westbrook of Misty Hollow?" Amy asked.

"Yes. Any information we found we gave directly to him."

"And when did you discover what happened to your brother Alex?"

A couple of days before Christmas." Tears welled in her eyes. "He was still recovering from his injuries. Since going to the hospital could possibly let Romano know he was still alive, he went into hiding and tended to his wounds himself. My brother is lucky to be alive."

"Yes, he is. The state would like to provide the evidence spoken about here to the jury." She resumed her seat as the bailiff gave copies of some of the files to the jury to be looked over.

A man behind Levi stood. A second later, a shot rang out. The bailiff fell.

The judge ducked behind the podium. The jury screamed and rushed for the door.

Mack threw herself to the floor as another shot rang out.

Levi leaped over the rail separating the front of the courtroom from the back and slid behind the pony wall Mack had taken cover behind. How had a gun gotten into the courtroom? His gaze met the frightened face of the judge. The bailiff had taken cover in the witness box.

"My room." The man jerked his head toward a door. "Think we can make it."

"The shooter didn't want to kill anyone. It's an attempt to rescue Romano." They couldn't let that happen. "Do you have a gun in that room?"

"Top right hand drawer of my desk. I've pressed the panic button. Help should be here within minutes."

Levi kissed Mack. "Stay down. I'll be right back."

He spotted the gunman removing a set of keys from the bailiff's belt. The bailiff's stomach rose and fell. Good. He was alive.

Levi ducked into the office, retrieved the gun, and stepped back into the courtroom. "Romano isn't going anywhere. Drop your weapon."

The man raised his weapon and stepped in front of

Romano. The double doors at the back of the courtroom burst open and four armed officers barged inside. When the gunman refused to drop his weapon, one of the officers fired.

The man dropped with a thud.

Romano held up his hands the best he could with his recovering wounds. Two officers stood on each side of him like stern bookends in an empty room.

The courtroom was cleared and adjourned to resume at a later date.

~

Three weeks later, Romano was found guilty on all counts. Instead of being rescued, his goon had sealed his boss's fate. Romano would spend the rest of his life in prison with no chance for parole.

"Where are we going to celebrate?" Alex asked.

"You know the city better than I do." Levi put an arm around Mack. It was finally over. He could tell her how he felt and ask her to stay.

"It's going to be good to get back to normal," she said.

His heart dropped. Normal meant her life in Little Rock, not Misty Hollow. Some of the pleasure of Romano's life sentence dimmed. He no longer cared about celebrating.

"Italian it is. A fitting choice." Alex grinned. "There's a great place just a couple of blocks from here. We can walk."

Mack wrapped her arms around Levi's waist, sending pain through his heart. "Thank you for being a hero. Again."

"It's what I do." He forced the words from a tortured throat. At her questioning look, he managed a smile. "I told you. I'm here for you whenever you need me." He wanted to be so much more than a friend and protector.

Alex watched them, then laughed, as if he had a secret busting to get out. "Come on, you two."

If he did have a secret, why keep it inside? Especially if it involved Mack? Levi would finagle the answer from his friend tonight one way or another. Secrets were what had forced them into the mess that almost got them killed.

No more.

Chapter Twenty

Mack hung up her suit and changed into fleece-lined leggings and a baggy sweatshirt. Now that the trial was over, she needed to make plans for the future. She moved to the window and watched the snow fall,

Would the roads be passable once the snow stopped? She and Alex might be stuck on the ranch for another few days or a week. Would that be a bad thing?

Her gaze landed on Levi heading for the garage. If she left, his life would return to normal. So would hers, actually. The law office would reopen. Since Romano's trial had hit all the papers and news channels, their business would be booming.

Still, her heart felt empty at the thought of leaving. Not the town so much. She hadn't been in Misty Hollow long enough to grow attached to the place or its people. But, she wasn't sure she wanted to leave Levi.

Mack glanced at the coffee table where the box containing the pen rested. She smiled. *Big Mack*. A name she'd once hated. Not anymore. Not after knowing Levi meant it as an affectionate nickname. What she didn't know was whether he looked at her now as more than the little sister of his best friend.

How could she find out short of outright asking? She sighed and stepped away from the window. Mrs. White would be expecting her in the kitchen to help prepare supper—something she really didn't enjoy. Cooking was definitely not part of her skill set.

She opened the door to see Alex standing there, hand raised in preparation to knock. "Where have you been?"

"In town." He grinned. "Got a minute?"

"The roads are passable?" She stepped back so he could enter, then she closed the door against the cold.

"For now. I doubt they will be by nightfall." He shrugged out of his coat and dropped it on the arm of the sofa.

Mack frowned and hung it on a hook by the door. "What's up?"

"Well." He sat on the sofa. "I've always considered myself an observant man."

"Yeah, so?" She sat across from him, wishing he'd get to the point so she could go help in the kitchen.

"It doesn't take much to see that you care about Levi."

"I've known him most of my life, Alex. Of course, I do." She crossed her arms. What was he getting at?

"How would you like to stay in Misty Hollow?"

"On the ranch?" She frowned. "I already have a job."

"I know that. I don't mean on the ranch, Mackenzie." He looked at her as if she were dense. "I rented an office in town. Thought it might be nice to set up a practice here. There isn't a lawyer in Misty

Hollow, and I'd be available to service all the neighboring small towns, too. What do you say?"

Stay? "You did this without asking me. When?"

"After that day in the warehouse. I could see how much you and Levi care about—"

"He's never said a word about having more feelings for me than he always has."

"I can tell." Alex grinned. "Don't you think a change would be nice after the whole Romano fiasco? Besides, how much trouble can I get into out here?"

"Where would we stay?" A bubble of excitement grew.

"I found us a house. It isn't much, but it'll do. What do you say?"

She jumped to her feet. "I say let's go to Little Rock and pack up our things. Have you told Levi?"

"Not yet. I wanted to tell you first. That way, if you didn't want to move here, I'd simply break the lease, and no one would be the wiser."

Mack threw her arms around her brother's neck. "Yes, I want to stay. Let me be the one to tell Levi. I need to see his reaction. Then I'll be able to tell whether the news is good news or bad."

"I'm pretty sure it'll be good news." He tightened the hug, then stepped back. "We can head into town as soon as the road is deemed safe. The snow doesn't look as if it'll stick around for long."

"Thank you for not dying." Mack grabbed her coat and sailed out the door. She'd be late to the kitchen, but she couldn't waste one more minute not knowing whether Levi cared for her as a woman or just as his friend's little sister.

He wasn't in the garage or the barn. When she

knocked on the bunkhouse door, Willy told her it was Levi's time to ride the perimeter of the ranch and that he'd be back by lunch.

Disappointment flooded through her as she headed for the main house. She wouldn't be able to speak privately to him for a couple of hours at least. If he didn't react favorably to the news, she'd tell Alex to break the lease and take her back to Little Rock. *Oh, Lord, let him be happy that she was staying.*

The warmth of the kitchen greeted her the moment she stepped inside. Mrs. White and Marilyn turned to face her, clapping. "Good job," Mrs. White said. "You got a bad man off the streets and live to tell the tale."

"Thank you. It does feel good." She exchanged her coat for an apron. "Sorry I'm late. My brother had some news."

"Good news, I hope." Marilyn peeled potatoes.

"I hope so." Mack picked up the other peeler. "Either way, I doubt we'll be on the ranch much longer. Maybe another day or two."

She turned to see a wide-eyed Levi standing in the doorway.

~

So, she was leaving. He whirled and marched back outside, hoping the cold would numb the pain in his heart.

Levi shoved his hands deep into his pockets. He still hadn't found the time to dig out of Alex what secret he was keeping, Maybe now was the time. It might keep his mind off the fact Mack would be leaving. At this point, he didn't care whether his friend's secret made him mad or not. He just needed something to replace the sadness that filled him after hearing Mack's words to Mrs. White.

He stomped up the two steps to Mack's front door and pounded his fist on the navy painted wood. "Alex, you in there?"

A sleepy Alex opened the door. "Yeah, what's all the commotion, dude? I'm trying to catch up on some much-needed sleep."

Levi stepped inside. "I came to find out what you've been keeping from me. Mind if I sit?" He motioned to a chair.

"Not at all. Want some coffee? I think there's still some in the pot."

"No, thanks." He lowered himself into a chair too small for his large frame. He watched as his friend poured himself a cup, then added cream and sugar. It was almost as if Alex was stalling. When he'd finished preparing his drink, he sat across from Levi.

"There's no need to worry, my friend. You'll probably like to hear what I've got to say. At least I hope so."

"Stop skirting the issue and tell me."

"Mack and I will be heading back to Little Rock in a couple of days."

"I heard." Levi's shoulders slumped. He leaned forward, dangling his hands between his knees. "I'm happy for you."

Alex frowned. "What's stuck in your craw? I thought you'd be happy."

Happy? How could he be happy that the woman he realized he loved more than as the little sister of Alex was leaving? "You've got to do what you've got to do." He pushed to his feet and thrust out his hand.

"Don't be a stranger. We let too much time pass and almost didn't get to reconnect."

Alex's brow furrowed as he stared at Levi's hand. "Okay. This sure didn't go the way I thought it would." He shook Levi's hand. "I have a few things to take care of here in Misty Hollow before heading to Little Rock, but that shouldn't take long. The snow doesn't look as if it will stick."

"No, it probably won't." Levi took a deep breath. "I really am glad you're alive. The world wouldn't be the same without you." His world wouldn't be the same without Mack.

Alex pulled him into a hug. "Neither me nor Mack would be here if you hadn't helped her. I owe you my life."

Levi returned the hug. "You're like a brother to me. I never gave it a second thought." He stepped back and clapped Alex on the shoulder. "Good luck. You know where to find me if you need me." Gut-wrenched, he returned to the cold outside. His gaze landed on the house where he could see the other ranch hands gathered around the dining table.

Mack set something on the table, then took her seat. Did it bother her that he wasn't there? Would she miss him when she left?

He thrust his hands deep into his pocket and headed for the barn. The presence of the horses always calmed him. Not so much this time. Despite their nickers of welcome, Levi had never felt more alone. What was he going to do? He'd grown used to seeing Mack every day, fighting for justice at her side, loving her as a man loves a woman.

He sat on a stool and rubbed his hands roughly

down his face. He hadn't shaved that morning. Stubble rasped against his palms. Who cared? Trucks and farm equipment didn't care one whit whether he shaved.

Realizing how ridiculous he acted, he pushed to his feet. He had no claim on Mackenzie Anderson. Never had. He hadn't told her of his feelings, his fault only, so why wouldn't she make plans for the future she could now have with Romano off the street?

A shadow darkened the doorway of the barn. He widened his eyes at the sight of Mack. Had she come to say goodbye? He took a deep breath and squared his shoulders. He would smile and wish her good luck, same as he had her brother. He moved toward her, stopping at the sight of her eyes welling with tears. "What's wrong?"

"You weren't at the meal."

"No, I'm not hungry."

"You're pulling away from me." She moved to within a few inches of him and peered into his face. "Now that Romano is locked up, I…well, I guess I didn't know what I thought, but it wasn't this. It wasn't you avoiding me."

"I'm not avoiding you."

"Then what is it?" A tear escaped.

He rubbed it away with his thumb. "You're leaving. I'm…preparing myself."

Confusion clouded her face. "I won't be gone long, Levi." The confusion fled to be replaced with amusement. Tears replaced by the twinkle of a smile. "What did you hear?"

"I heard you tell Mrs. White you were going back to Little Rock. Alex confirmed the news." Had he heard wrong?

"To get our things, Levi." She moved close enough for him to feel the heat of her body. "We're staying in Misty Hollow. Alex is opening his law office here. What did he tell you?"

"Uh." He raked his brain to recall the conversation. Levi had eluded to the idea that he knew what Alex had planned. Alex had assumed he already knew. A laugh escaped him. "A simple miscommunication on my part." He wrapped his arms around her waist and pulled her against him.

"Are you happy I'm staying?" Her gaze locked with his.

"Darlin', I couldn't be happier. I should've come to you, but I wanted to wait until the Romano danger was behind us before I told you of my feelings for you."

"What are they?" Her whisper wafted across his face.

"I love you, Mackenzie. I always have. What I felt as a boy, your protector, has grown to be the fire a man feels for a woman he wants to spend the rest of his life with."

The tears returned to her eyes. "A lot of years have passed. You don't really know the woman, only the child."

He smiled. "Oh, I think I do. The woman is as beautiful inside as out. She's brave, desires justice, will take on a bear to protect the ones she loves. Dare I hope that I am one of them?"

"Oh, Levi." She rested her cheek against his chest. "I've loved you from the first time you walked through the door as a teen. You've always been more than the friend of my brother. At least to me. When Alex told me of his news, I was so happy. Then, you didn't come to supper. I thought you didn't want me to stay."

He cupped her face. "My world was ending when I thought you were leaving." He lowered his face and showed her the best way he could just how happy he was that she was staying.

Epilogue

The early days of spring beckoned Levi and Mack to the overlook on Misty Mountain that gave them a view of the morning mist hiding the town far below them. Mack leaned against Levi. Neither of them spoke, not wanting to dispel the peace of the morning.

The last few months had been spent establishing the law office in town and she and Levi getting to know each other better without the threat of danger dogging their heels. Mack couldn't be happier at her brother's decision or hers to join him. She couldn't imagine her life without her brother or the man she loved.

"This is the most beautiful thing I've ever seen," she said softly.

"Oh, I've seen something more beautiful."

She turned in his arms to face him. "Oh?"

"She's in my arms right now." He set her at arm's length away. "Watch, sweetheart."

"Okay." Disappointment pricked her heart. She'd really thought today would be the day he proposed. She sighed and turned to watch the sun kiss away the mist with lips of rose and lavender as it rose in the sky.

"Mackenzie Anderson."

She turned to see Levi on one knee. Tears sprang to her eyes. Her heart leaped.

"I'm asking you to marry me. Right here at this lookout. I'm proposing as the sun rises, but I'd like to marry you as the sun sets to begin the rest of our life. Will you marry me?" He opened a little black box to reveal a diamond ring. "Will you wear my grandmother's ring?"

She fell to her knees in front of him. "Of course, I will, Levi Owens. I'd be honored to be Mackenzie Big Mack Owens." She held out her left hand and choked back a sob as he slid the ring on her finger. "When?"

"Sunset next Saturday. Something small? Those from the ranch and Alex?"

She nodded. With no family other than her brother, a big wedding seemed unnecessary. Nothing could be more perfect than being married on Misty Mountain surrounded by friends with the view of the valley behind them. "Sounds absolutely perfect to me." Placing her hands on his shoulders, she pushed to her feet. "Stand up and seal your proposal with a kiss before I change my mind." She smiled through her tears.

He laughed and stood. "Bossy as usual. Don't ever change." He lowered his head and claimed her lips in a kiss so sweet it had only existed in her dreams. A kiss now made real. A kiss of promise.

The End

www.cynthiahickey.com

Cynthia Hickey is a multi-published and best-selling author of cozy mysteries and romantic suspense. She has taught writing at many conferences and small writing retreats. She and her husband run the publishing press, Winged Publications. They live in Arizona and Arkansas, becoming snowbirds with three dogs. They have ten grandchildren who keep them busy and tell everyone they know that "Nana is a writer."

Connect with me on FaceBook
Twitter
Sign up for my newsletter and receive a free short story
www.cynthiahickey.com

Follow me on Amazon
And Bookbub
Shop my bookstore on shopify. For better price and autographed books. You can also subscribe to Mysterious Delivery, a mystery and suspense monthly book subscription with a book and several surprise goodies to pamper the reader.

Enjoy other books by Cynthia Hickey

Cowboys of Misty Hollow

Cowboy Jeopardy
Cowboy Peril
Cowboy Hazard
Cowgirl Blaze
Cowboy Uncertainty

Misty Hollow
Secrets of Misty Hollow
Deceptive Peace
Calm Surface
Lightning Never Strikes Twice
Lethal Inheritance
Bitter Isolation
Say I Don't
Christmas Stalker
Bridge to Safety
When Night Falls
A Place to Hide
Mountain Refuge

Stay in Misty Hollow for a while. Get the entire series here!

The Seven Deadly Sins series
Deadly Pride
Deadly Covet
Deadly Lust
Deadly Glutton
Deadly Envy
Deadly Sloth
Deadly Anger

COWBOY CHRISTMAS CRISIS

The Tail Waggin' Mysteries
Cat-Eyed Witness
The Dog Who Found a Body
Troublesome Twosome
Four-Legged Suspect
Unwanted Christmas Guest
Wedding Day Cat Burglar

Brothers Steele
Sharp as Steele
Carved in Steele
Forged in Steele
Brothers Steele (All three in one)

The Brothers of Copper Pass
Wyatt's Warrant
Dirk's Defense
Stetson's Secret
Houston's Hope
Dallas's Dare
Seth's Sacrifice
Malcolm's Misunderstanding
The Brothers of Copper Pass Boxed Set

Time Travel
The Portal

Tiny House Mysteries
No Small Caper
Caper Goes Missing
Caper Finds a Clue

Caper's Dark Adventure
A Strange Game for Caper
Caper Steals Christmas
Caper Finds a Treasure
Tiny House Mysteries boxed set

Wife for Hire – Private Investigators
Saving Sarah
Lesson for Lacey
Mission for Meghan
Long Way for Lainie
Aimed at Amy
Wife for Hire (all five in one)

A Hollywood Murder
Killer Pose, book 1
Killer Snapshot, book 2
Shoot to Kill, book 3
Kodak Kill Shot, book 4
To Snap a Killer
Hollywood Murder Mysteries

Shady Acres Mysteries
Beware the Orchids, book 1
Path to Nowhere
Poison Foliage
Poinsettia Madness
Deadly Greenhouse Gases
Vine Entrapment
Shady Acres Boxed Set

CLEAN BUT GRITTY Romantic Suspense

Highland Springs

Murder Live
Say Bye to Mommy
To Breathe Again
Highland Springs Murders (all 3 in one)

Colors of Evil Series

Shades of Crimson
Coral Shadows

The Pretty Must Die Series

Ripped in Red, book 1
Pierced in Pink, book 2
Wounded in White, book 3
Worthy, The Complete Story

Lisa Paxton Mystery Series

Eenie Meenie Miny Mo
Jack Be Nimble
Hickory Dickory Dock
Boxed Set

Hearts of Courage
A Heart of Valor
The Game
Suspicious Minds
After the Storm

Local Betrayal
Hearts of Courage Boxed Set

Overcoming Evil series
Mistaken Assassin
Captured Innocence
Mountain of Fear
Exposure at Sea
A Secret to Die for
Collision Course
Romantic Suspense of 5 books in 1

INSPIRATIONAL

Nosy Neighbor Series
Anything For A Mystery, Book 1
A Killer Plot, Book 2
Skin Care Can Be Murder, Book 3
Death By Baking, Book 4
Jogging Is Bad For Your Health, Book 5
Poison Bubbles, Book 6
A Good Party Can Kill You, Book 7
Nosy Neighbor collection

Christmas with Stormi Nelson

The Summer Meadows Series
Fudge-Laced Felonies, Book 1
Candy-Coated Secrets, Book 2
Chocolate-Covered Crime, Book 3
Maui Macadamia Madness, Book 4

All four novels in one collection

The River Valley Mystery Series
Deadly Neighbors, Book 1
Advance Notice, Book 2
The Librarian's Last Chapter, Book 3
All three novels in one collection

Historical cozy
Hazel's Quest

Historical Romances
Runaway Sue
Taming the Sheriff
Sweet Apple Blossom
A Doctor's Agreement
A Lady Maid's Honor
A Touch of Sugar
Love Over Par
Heart of the Emerald
A Sketch of Gold
Her Lonely Heart

Finding Love the Harvey Girl Way
Cooking With Love
Guiding With Love
Serving With Love
Warring With Love
All 4 in 1

Finding Love in Disaster
The Rancher's Dilemma
The Teacher's Rescue
The Soldier's Redemption

Woman of courage Series

A Love For Delicious
Ruth's Redemption
Charity's Gold Rush
Mountain Redemption
They Call Her Mrs. Sheriff
Woman of Courage series

Short Story Westerns
Flowers of the Desert

Contemporary

Romance in Paradise
Maui Magic
Sunset Kisses
Deep Sea Love
3 in 1

Finding a Way Home
Service of Love
Hillbilly Cinderella
Unraveling Love
I'd Rather Kiss My Horse

Christmas

Dear Jillian

Romancing the Fabulous Cooper Brothers

Handcarved Christmas

The Payback Bride

Curtain Calls and Christmas Wishes

Christmas Gold

A Christmas Stamp

Snowflake Kisses

Merry's Secret Santa

A Christmas Deception

The Red Hat's Club (Contemporary novellas)

Finally

Suddenly

Surprisingly

The Red Hat's Club 3 – in 1

Short Story

One Hour (A short story thriller)

Whisper Sweet Nothings (a Valentine short romance)

CYNTHIA HICKEY

Made in the USA
Monee, IL
05 October 2024

67237913R00105